The Academy Series
Book 8 – Surprised Beyond Belief

My Gratitude: Hello my sexy readers! I'm beyond blessed to have your support and the numerous positive emails that I continue to receive. I appreciate you all more than you know! Now on to the good stuff...

I'm very excited to bring you book 8 - "Surprised Beyond Belief" in "The Academy" series. This book doesn't miss a beat and picks up right where book 7 - "Inappropriate Behavior" left off.

I've worked diligently to ensure each book can standalone and can still be enjoyed without reading the previous books in this series. However, like many of the most successful stories ever released, such as Star Wars, Marvel, Harry Potter, Twilight, The Fast and the Furious, etc. It has more impact when the entire sequence of stories is followed in order.

If you are like me…. And want more than just a SLAP here and SPANK there, you will appreciate the back stories of these characters, their personalities, and their kinks. For this reason, I highly recommend that you read the entire books from this series in order, from 1 to 8. It will further entice and add to your reading experience. Plus, there will be several twists and turns that you might not expect…. SO I HOPE YOU'RE READY!

Please note: If bare bottom spanking, discipline, kinky sex, adult toys, threesomes, BDSM, that involves Male/female, Female/female, Female/male and numerous combinations of these, are not your thing, please don't buy, download, or read this book. It is not intended for you... Otherwise, congratulations! You may have just found your new favorite spanking book and erotic series!

As always I am truly grateful for your comments and positive reviews, as these are very helpful on all digital platforms.

Please feel free to say hi and join my mailing list at robinfairchild_author@yahoo.com. You'll receive FREE books and substantial discount promotions as well.

If you're a true spanking enthusiast, and love spanking as much as I do, then you will love reading my other books. I release new books often, so always check my website www.robinfairchild.com.

Love, Blessings, & Spanks,
Robin
xoxoxo

Recap

The semester is in full swing at The Academy, the prestigious private boarding college for gifted athletes, who are also equally brilliant scholars. The picturesque college in the quaint, charming town of Kentville, Connecticut, remains practically undetectable as it's nestled high in the hills and surrounded by farms owned by the founding sisters, Marilyn and Marjorie Devlin.

Even though The Academy maintains a low profile, those that do know about it are very familiar with its history. It is consistently ranked among the top 20 boarding schools in the country. The school continues to operate pretty much the same as it did since its inception. It focuses on strict old-fashioned values with a zero-tolerance policy for misbehavior. The minimum age to attend The Academy is 18, and due to it being very prestigious and in-demand, the tuition is very expensive.

The small college has a successful track record of its graduates that speaks for itself. It's known for producing some of the most intelligent and respected sports doctors, naturopathic doctors, coaches, and trainers in the country. In addition, it has spawned some amazing professional athletes, fitness models, and even Olympian athletes.

Many things about the small boarding college are quite unique. It has an all-female staff, its own dedicated security team, and luxurious living arrangements, where each student has their own apartment on campus. Perhaps the most unique thing about The Academy is the manner in which misbehaved and errant students are dealt with. The school maintains a very strict, no-nonsense policy in which bare bottom spankings are administered as the primary method of punishment.

For the past few years, the school has been operating under the direction of Principal Katherine "Kate" Kensington. The founding sisters themselves would be the first to admit that Principal Kate, who is an absolutely stunning, vibrant 34-year old woman, mom, and an ex-athlete herself, is the one responsible for skyrocketing The Academy to an even more prestigious, star status among small private boarding colleges.

Principal Kate is an extremely loving and nurturing woman, but she's an equally strict and very capable disciplinarian. Needless to say, that every teacher on her staff is also quite capable and never hesitant about dishing out the discipline when needed.

Among the female staff, there are two other amazing women that play a key role in assisting Principal Kate. It is very common for Kate to lean on them in the day-to-day operations of running the school and dealing with wayward students. These two women, Nurse Madison, and Jenn Summers, really play a huge role and have also contributed greatly to the success of The Academy.

The founding sisters, Ms. Marilyn and Ms. Marjorie are still quite involved in many things regarding the school, but they have been focusing their attention on running their farms, which have blossomed to be more successful than they could have ever imagined. Major investments such as hiring the best campus security team that money can buy, and making state-of-the-art renovations when needed, are more of what they have been concentrating their efforts on.

Both sisters are ecstatic at the way Principal Kate runs the school. She is totally dedicated and her no-nonsense philosophy is a perfect match to everything the two sisters believe in. They love how she maintains the same old fashion values they had established years ago. The Academy has and will always operate on these values with zero tolerance for misbehaving students.

All students have to be at least 18 years old to attend the school. They are required to read and sign the school handbook, as well as, the education contract, & consent form before enrollment. All parents and guardians must read and sign as well, even though at age 18 in Connecticut you are considered a legal adult. All the rules and school guidelines are explained in detail in this student handbook. It clearly states that any teacher or faculty member has the authority to use corporal punishment to discipline a student for infractions and misbehavior. This means anything such as poor grades, skipping school, work infractions, rudeness, disrespect, breaking curfew, drinking and missing workouts to name a few. With a zero tolerance policy, any student caught with narcotics, performance enhancing drugs, steroids, or convicted of a crime will be automatically expelled, and the tuition paid is forfeited.

The students totally understand the strict guidelines of the school. They constantly praise and respect the faculty for being loving & nurturing women that really care about them. However, they also understand these women all have a very stern side that falls in line with the school's no-nonsense approach.

Each teacher, along with Nurse Madison, has been properly trained in the various methods of handling & disciplining students. Every student knows that each of these loving but stern women has been given the reform school strap and the official school wooden paddle to use on them. It also states they will be suspended or even permanently kicked out of the college for any serious offenses.

Chapter 1

It's been an extremely busy past couple of months since the start of the semester. The prestigious college has gone through a few growing pains, which included several arrests for students selling and/or possessing narcotics. For some reason, Principal Kate has even felt that this semester has resulted in having her and her staff administering more discipline to misbehaved students than in the past several years.

Maybe it's because there are now video cameras all over the campus and the new security team has been nothing less than stellar at helping enforce the school's rules and regulations. There have also been several other things that have been uncharacteristic for Principal Kate this semester. She has been completely smitten and fell over Jordan Thompson, a handsome new first year student.

Not only does Jordan have the looks of a model and the physique of a super-hero, his personality is magnetic, and his charisma is something that Principal Kate can't ignore. To say that she really feels something for Jordan would be an understatement. She actually can't deny that it was love from the moment that she met him during the school's orientation. Since then, there has definitely been a great deal of flirting and some very close calls that could have resulted in fireworks much more explosive than the fourth of July.

Jordan, for some reason, seems to have that effect on most of the girls on campus. Of course, his amazing looks play a part, but he also has a somewhat mysterious side to him that drives them wild. Just about every girl on campus is vying for his attention. Jordan probably could have a date every night of the week if he wants to, but the cool thing about him is that he doesn't act on that, and just remains down-to-earth. He remains in a non-exclusive relationship with a feisty, second-year student, Julia, who like many of the other girls on campus, is totally hot and heavy over him. Not only has Jordan captured the attention of Principal Kate, Julia, and several other college cuties, he's harvesting a huge secret as well.

What no one else knows is that he and Nurse Madison have been involved in a wild, kinky, sex-crazy affair since the first week that school started. So far, they have been beyond careful to keep their relationship hidden from the outside world despite spending so much time spanking and fucking each other's brains out!

Being the new student on campus with those killer looks and that irresistible personality, has made Jordan stand out more than normal. Much to Ms. Marjorie's dismay, Jordan is here on a scholarship granted to him by her sister, Ms. Marilyn.

Ms. Marjorie makes it perfectly clear to the staff that she isn't a fan of the handsome new student, and has even questioned whether he could be the reason, or at least involved in some way, for the increasing number of crimes on campus.

So, needless to say, that Principal Kate, along with the founding sisters, and the new security team are doing all they can to keep the campus as safe and crime free as possible.

Principal Kate's been focused so much on this task, that aside from a few simple "hello's", she has been doing a pretty good job of avoiding Jordan. She realizes that if she ever got to be alone with him, fireworks would surely go off! As usual, Jordan has been a model student, and much to Principal Kate's dismay, hasn't even come close to getting into any kind of trouble.

In fact, the last two weeks have been super busy for Principal Kate, Nurse Madison, and the new campus security team. With the new personal search guidelines in place, a number of students have been strip searched and disciplined for having marijuana on them. Principal Kate and Nurse Madison are the key players in handling these types of infractions and disciplining those wayward students.

On a more serious note, two more students have been arrested and kicked out of school for possessing and using performance-enhancing drugs. Ms. Marilyn is still quite concerned and knows this is a huge issue on campus. However, she is more than satisfied with her investment in the new campus security team. So far, it has really paid off. They have done wonders in dealing with the major, more serious, problems on campus such as selling narcotics, cocaine, steroids, and other hard drugs. They continue to work hard and strive to keep the campus drug free.

On the positive side, spunky student Julia, is a model student this semester. Her grades have been outstanding, and she's kept her temper and her feisty nature in check. Jordan has been one of the key reasons for keeping her in line, even though they still aren't in an exclusive relationship, he's been holding her accountable for her actions and giving her the discipline that she needs and craves.

It's safe to say, that there's not a week or two that goes by when Jordan doesn't strip her down and totally dominate her. He not only reddens her cheeks but he also fucks her senseless, including his favorite, anal sex. He truly loves reaming her adorable ass with his cock. The other major reason why Julia is continuing to stay on the straight and narrow path is her close relationship with Nurse Madison.

Of course, no one other than Jordan, knows that Nurse Madison has been secretly mentoring Julia one-on-one, behind closed doors. The stunning nurse has really helped the young student develop more confidence within her own body. She especially helped Julia with regard to her sexual skills, intimacy, and performance. This one-on-one coaching from Nurse Madison, along with taking in all of Jordan's kinky antics, has really made Julia a total dynamo in bed. Jordan can attest to that, as well as Julia's friend-with benefits, Rebecca. Their kinky friendship often has them exploring each others body with no inhibitions. Even though Julia doesn't want to share Jordan with anyone, she'll put that aside because one of her ultimate fantasies is to experience a threesome.

In fact, her birthday is on Saturday and Jordan has already been teasing her all week that he plans to give her one hell of a birthday spanking, before fucking her every way imaginable. Julia had been giving it right back to him and equally teasing him as well. She's been bantering with him for weeks that she plans on having a threesome for her birthday. She'd been enticing him that when he goes over to her apartment on Saturday night that she might not be alone.

Hearing her hint and teasing him with the idea of this threesome, especially with the cute, blonde Rebecca, makes his dick swell to epic proportions. Julia tells Jordan just about everything, so he knows all about her and Rebecca's kinky, extra-curricular friendship. Of course, he totally approves. What guy wouldn't? The next step, and ultimate scenario, is to get them all together for an all-out fuck festival!

Saturday finally arrives with anticipation and after a morning workout, doing some homework, Jordan's just waking-up from a much need power nap. He is really looking forward to tonight and making Julia's 20th birthday as special as possible. He's made plans on taking her to her favorite restaurant, which is an upscale, quaint bistro on the outskirts of town. He grabs his cell phone and calls her.

"Happy birthday again, you cute, hot, sexy, adorable, mess! I can't wait to see you!"

"Haha!" Julia laughs, "Thank you, baby. I can't wait to see you too!"

"I'll pick you up at 7:30? We have reservations at 8."

Julia chimes back, "I want you here at 6pm, and bring that sexy toy bag of yours. You promised me a birthday spanking, among other things, and I plan on being a really bad girl tonight."

"Haha!" Jordan laughs into his phone, "Oh don't you worry, baby. Not only am I going to spank you, I'm going to fuck your brains out… Before and after dinner. And since you've been hinting about a threesome for your birthday, I'll make sure Rebecca and I double team you good and give you a night you'll never forget!"

Julia chimes back with a laugh, "Haha! Wow! You're so sure that's what is going down? I guess I haven't concealed it very well."

"You've been teasing me for the past couple of weeks about having a threesome. And, Rebecca's been hinting, flirting, and looking me up and down these past few days, like I'm a piece of meat," Jordan chuckles.

"Well, she always wanted you, and tonight I'm giving her the go ahead." Julia giggled. "It's time and we've been teasing you like crazy. I'm really looking forward to it myself. I can't ask for a better birthday present than to have both of you, who I really love so much!"

Jordan chuckled, "Have it your way, baby. I'll give you everything you want and more… See you at 6, with my bag of toys."

"Oh, I plan on having it my way!" Julia replied, "Don't be late or

Rebecca and I might have to spank you."

Jordan smiles from ear to ear as their phone call comes to an end. His cock is throbbing like a sub-woofer in a dance club. It won't be the first threesome in his life, but it's sure to be one hell of a memory fucking the daylights out of firecracker Julia, and equally hot, Rebecca together, at the same time!

Jordan heads into the shower to get ready for the date. He's doing all he can not to stroke himself and relieve the gargantuan sized hard-on he's sprouting right now. He pauses long enough to look into the mirror and snaps a picture of himself fully naked with that elephantine dick of his. He then sends a text to Nurse Madison, cleverly disguised as Aunt Mary on his cell phone.

"Hey Aunt Mary, just saying hi. Are you there?"

She texted back.
"Hi honey, I'm here. I'm actually getting ready for a date. How are you? Are you all set to take Julia out for her birthday?"

"Yep, I'm getting ready now. The way you've been coaching her and showing her the ropes, has really made her so confident. She's a total sex maniac, just like you! I'm sure you know all about her plans for our threesome."

"Let's just say that Julia is a girl that knows what she wants and goes for it. You're in for a memorable night."

Jordan texted his reply, *"I wish you were a part of it. Rebecca is cute but I would love to have you and Julia at the same time."*

"Well, you never know. That may just happen one day!" Nurse Madison teases back, *"Have fun and give it to them good... Lol!"*

"ABSOLUTELY!" Jordan texted back using all uppercase. He then sends Madison the selfie snapshot of his beautiful physique, posed in front of his mirror, complete with that incredible erection.

"God, that body of yours is so amazing! Save some for me. The guy I'm dating is taking me to a play...boring! He's attractive, older, 58, but unfortunately, he's dull. He definitely doesn't have a dick like yours! See ya tomorrow? I plan on sucking that cock of yours like a lollipop... Lol"

"For sure, can't wait to see you." Jordan replied back and attached several smiley face and heart emoji's. He then quickly deleted the history of text messages between them.

He proceeded to take his shower and get all decked out for their hot evening. He grabbed his gym bag stuffed with sex toys, implements, lube, and everything else imaginable and headed to Julia's apartment. Within a few minutes, he arrived and knocked on her door.

Chapter 2

Julia opened the door to greet him and was immediately welcomed with a beautiful bouquet of red roses.

"Happy Birthday!" Jordan chimed, as her pretty face smiled with delight.

His big green eyes opened wide to take in how absolutely beautiful she looked with her long fire-red hair done up with soft, flowing curls. She wasn't even fully dressed as she welcomed him wrapped in a large bath towel. She was holding a couple of make-up brushes, foundation, and lipstick in her hands.

"Aw! Thank you, babe!" she hugged him tightly.

She quickly put the items in her hands down on the table, and took hold of the roses. Julia planted a very passionate and sexy kiss on that handsome face of his.

"I just finished my hair. Do you like it? I'm half-way through doing my make-up. Then I'll get dressed."

"I love it! You are breathtakingly beautiful." Jordan commented, then smirked. "You should wait until after I spank you to finish your make-up. You might be bawling your eyes out."

"Haha!" Julia chuckles, "Might be?... I always cry a river when you spank me, but I totally love it... And, I need it!"

"In that case, let's get right to it, young lady." Jordan replied as he yanked the towel off her super-sexy, petite, body.

Julia's cute, very toned, physique was as appetizing as it gets as she stood naked before him. Jordan took one look at her glistening under the soft lighting in her apartment and then hoisted her up and held her close to him. Julia wrapped her strong legs around his waist as their tongues collided into another sexy, passion-filled kiss.

After several minutes of devouring each other, Jordan placed her back on her feet.

"I want you to open this first," Jordan told her as he handed her a small, beautifully wrapped box.

Julia's eyes lit up, as she placed the roses down and took hold of the gift. She opened it and smiled from ear to ear as she stared at the stunning silver necklace with a heart pendant.

"Oh my God, babe! It's beautiful! You didn't have to get me anything. You're taking me to dinner and the roses…That's more than enough."

"Even though we agree not to be exclusive as boyfriend and girlfriend, I want this to be a reminder of how special you are to me. You'll always have a place in my heart, no matter what."

"Jordan, I'm gonna cry… And, it's not from your spanking." Julia's eyes teared up hearing those sincere words come out of his mouth.

Jordan gently turns her around and fastens the shiny silver necklace around her neck. Of course, he takes in the view of her amazing little bubble of an ass, then softly pats it a few times with the palm of his right hand.

"You're going to give me my birthday spankings now, aren't you sir?" Julia says to him in her innocent but sexy playful voice as she turns her head and looks over her left shoulder at Jordan.

She can't help but notice the way he's staring her body down. His eyes are especially focused and glued onto her ass cheeks. He has that look of a wild animal that's ready to pounce and devour its prey. It's that look, that feeling, that every girl wants their guy to have towards them. That feeling of being totally desirable. Julia gets that feeling from Jordan all the time and she absolutely loves it. In return, she's not shy and doesn't hesitate to give that same sexy, desirable look right back to him as her body quivers with anticipation. She also loves the way he totally takes control and doesn't hold back one bit from being aggressive and manhandling her. She knows that it's a matter of seconds before he really goes to town on her hiney, then fucks her into the hemisphere.

"You know I'm going to give you much more than just a birthday spanking. Especially since you went out drinking with Rebecca two nights ago," Jordan replied in his stern, deep voice.

"I accept my punishment, sir," Julia chimed back, "Can I just request that you give me some of it now, and more of it after dinner? I want to feel that anticipation, knowing that I'm going to get more later tonight. I may never want this night to end."

"Should I even ask how you want me to spank you?" Jordan chuckled a bit.

"I know how much you love using the leather strap on me and watching me dance from leg to leg. Maybe we can save that for after dinner?... I told you all about the way Principal Kate spanked me last year for fighting with Cassie. March me into my bedroom and redden my cheeks!"

"You are one sexy bitch!... And, way too sexy for your own good!" Jordan replied as he forcefully took hold of her, "Let's go Missy!... Move it!"

His right hand forcefully grabbed onto her left earlobe, making her head immediately tilt to the left. His left arm applied a vice-like grip on her bicep. That force, that feeling of being manhandled, instantly made Julia's vagina flow with wetness.

Julia felt his force with every step as he marched her towards the bedroom. Jordan skillfully remembered every vivid detail that Julia shared with him on the way Principal Kate spanked her that day at Ms. Marilyn's house, including the exact position that the sexy but stern principal spanked her in.

At age 19, it was the first spanking that Julia ever received, and boy, it sure was a doozy! Principal Kate administered a relentless hand spanking, bare bottom, right in front of The Academy's founder, Ms. Marilyn. As it turns out, it was much more than just a spanking, it served as the catalyst for Julia's sexual awakening.

Within seconds, they entered Julia's bedroom. Jordan cleverly marched her to a position right in front of her full-length mirror. He knew that Julia had many sides to her sexuality. So, by looking in the mirror and seeing herself getting a relentless spanking, it would definitely hit a nerve with her, and make it memorable for sure.

Jordan remained standing and pulled Julia into position, slightly bent-over his left hip. Of course, there's no way that he can compare with the sexy, curvy hips of Principal Kate, but his strength is undeniable. He quickly secured Julia by tightly wrapping his left arm around her waist as his right hand began to rain down on her pretty little ass.

<SLAP><SLAP><SLAP><SLAP>

Julia let out a loud cry as her cheeks were greeted with the familiarity of his strong right hand.

<SLAP><SLAP><SLAP>
<SLAP><SLAP>
<SLAP><SLAP><SLAP><SLAP>

"Oow!… OUCH!" Julia bawled, as her watery eyes continued to look in the mirror to take in every second of this spanking.

She not only got to see that stern, no-nonsense look on Jordan's face, she also got to watch how her pale white cheeks became instantly swollen and covered in red with his hand prints. Julia couldn't help it as she danced and squirmed over his hip. Even though each of her legs would come off the floor, kicking in an alternate pattern, Jordan was un-phased. His eyes remained glued to the prize… her adorable volleyball-shaped ass!

<SLAP>
<SLAP><SLAP>
<SLAP><SLAP><SLAP><SLAP><SLAP>

Jordan delivered the last flurry of this hand spanking, then released her and spun her around to scold her.

"Let this be a lesson not to go out drinking. And when we get home, you're going to get a serious strapping. Is that understood, young lady?"

Julia's hands immediately began rubbing her cheeks, as she mumbled the words, "Yes sir!"

Her sparkling eyes flowed with so many tears that it made her mascara run down her face. Jordan wiped the black stains from her face and then gave her another one of his famous sexy kisses.

"You are one sexy mother-fucker," Julia replied, when they came up for air, "and, one hell of a spanker!… God, I love the way you discipline me!"

Her confession through those water-filled, pretty blue eyes of hers made him smile from ear to ear. Julia then dropped to her knees and wasted no time in unbuttoning his stylish, black dress pants. She quickly yanked them down to the floor along with his underwear. Of course, Jordan's massive cock was completely erect and pointing toward the ceiling. Julia looked at it with that burning desire as she took hold of it and guided it into her mouth.

Jordan's head tilted back as he felt the warmth of her tongue licking him like an ice-cream cone. Julia's petite hands cupped and then squeezed his testicles with a nice firm grip. She then paid attention to each one individually, fondling and squeezing them with the perfect amount of pressure. All this was happening at the same time that her mouth was literally devouring his dick. Jordan was in heaven as her blow job felt amazing.

Julia then took it a step further. She reached her right hand behind him and firmly dug her fingernails into his left ass cheek. Jordan responded with a slight yelp as she gave him a good hard pinch that felt like several bee stings. Jordan knew this perfect combination of pleasure and pain all too well. After all, he's been getting the blow jobs of his life weekly from Nurse Madison. It was obvious that Julia was also benefiting greatly from her time alone with the sexy nurse, and the one-on-one mentoring that she'd been giving her. The way she was blowing Jordan was following the exact same pattern that Nurse Madison uses when her mouth engulfs his dick.

Julia continued to keep him on cloud nine as she now pulled and held his entire body tightly in her mouth. Her pretty little hands spread his ass cheeks and her right index finger began to tease his asshole. After about half a minute of teasing him, Julia plunged her finger into his rectum. Jordan's breathing immediately changed and became even more labored. His sexy moans gave her all the confirmation she needed to know that her oral skills and everything she was doing to him was spot on.

Julia could have easily continued for a few more minutes and blown Jordan into ecstasy, but she had even more plans for him right now.

"Don't you dare cum. I want that dick inside me," she told him as she freed his rock-hard dick from her mouth.

"Strip...get out of those clothes, baby." She then whispered in a sexy voice as she removed her finger from his drilling his rectum.

Within a few seconds, Jordan removed every stitch of clothing from his body as they fell into another passion-filled kiss.

"Talk about being a sexy mother-fucker!" Jordan commented, "I thought you wanted to wait until after dinner?"

"I plan on having you now, AND, when we get home," Julia replied with emphasis, "You're not the only one that has toys in your closet."

Julia walked with purpose towards her bedroom closet and opened the door. She then reached inside and pulled out a surprise she'd been dying to try. Jordan's head kicked back and his eyes blinked hard.

"What the?" He reacted.

Chapter 3

Julia's arm was gripped tightly onto the arm of Trevor, a cute, muscular, first-year student. She pulled him into the center of her bedroom. Trevor was also completely naked as his body was slightly trembling.

"I told you I wanted a threesome for my birthday and I meant it!" Julia announced as she looked at Jordan.

"Babe, I don't go that way... I'm straight." Jordan replied.

"So am I, dude!" Trevor quickly piped back, "You think I want you?... Fuck no, I want her!"

"It's not about either of you... It's about me," Julia replied, "I know you both are straight and I'm not expecting you to do anything to each other... but I am expecting you both to double-team me, and fuck my brains out!"

Julia's bold response stuns Jordan as she now kneels down and starts blowing Trevor. It takes only a matter of seconds of using her amazing oral skills on him to get his cock as hard as a baseball bat. Julia then reverses the position as she stands up and pushes Trevor down to his knees.

"Lick my pussy!" She commands Trevor, and then looks over to Jordan, "And you... kiss me like only you know how to do."

Trevor begins to go down on her and Jordan gives her exactly what she asked for. He kisses her with that fire in his eyes as he firmly tugs on her long, curly, red hair. Julia's sexy moans fill her bedroom as Jordan now moves on to kissing her neck and shoulders. He then traces his tongue all the way down her spine.

"Ahh!" Julia basks in the sensation of two hot guys totally working her over with their tongues.

Jordan's talented tongue & plush lips continue to work their magic as he now starts kissing and licking every inch of her pretty ass that he has just reddened. Julia bends over to give Jordan even better access, knowing he's about to rim her good. She directs Trevor to exactly where she wants his tongue to lick and tease her clitoris.

"Right Here, Trev..." She calls out, "Ah... Yes!"

Jordan now plunges his tongue inside her ass as his strong hand pulls her cheeks apart as far as possible. Julia moans loudly as she feels his sexy tongue enter her rectum and rim like he's done countless times to her.

"Oh... Fuck, Yes! Mmmm, that feels so good, baby!" She lets Jordan know how amazing it feels.

After a good while of literally getting her licks, Julia signals them to follow her. She gets on her bed and kneels on all fours. She motions Jordan to position him on the opposite side of the bed and then lets him know what she wants.

"I want that cock of yours back in my mouth, baby!" She tells him, and then looks over at Trevor and instructs him as well, "You, put a condom on... and fuck me hard!... And make sure you still pull out. We still need to play it safe in case the condom breaks... Now fuck me with everything you got, Trevor!"

Within a matter of seconds, Jordan's dick enters her mouth as Trevor's cock begins to ram her pussy. She's right back to blowing Jordan exactly the way he wants it. She pauses for a second and calls out.

"Harder Trevor!" Julia coaches him and then continues sucking Jordan's dick and fondling his balls.

"Mmmm!" Is about all she manages to muster as Trevor really starts to fuck her hard the way she wanted. His hands grab onto her hips as he really puts everything he has into each thrust.

"Ahh! Mmmm! You feel amazing!" came from Trevor's mouth.

"Harder Trevor... Fuck me harder!" Julia called out.

Julia is so used to getting the daylights fucked out of her by Jordan that even though Trevor is giving her a good, hard pounding, he's just not at Jordan's skill level. Trevor continues to maintain a vigorous pace and within another minute, he pulls out of her vagina and moans, "Mmmm... I'm coming!"

Julia refrains for a moment from tending to Jordan, and spins around to make sure Trevor really gets off. She grabs the shaft of his dick with her pretty hands and strokes him vigorously, making sure that every last drop of sperm fills the condom.

Trevor's entire body tenses up as he moans with delight. Jordan just smirks as he looks on from the opposite side of the bed. He knows Julia has become a total sexual firecracker who is full-on amazing in bed! Not only has Nurse Madison played a huge role in getting her to this point, so did he as well.

Jordan, was the one to not only hold her accountable and discipline her with bare bottom spankings, he was also the person that introduced her to so many aspects of BDSM. He used everything from restraints, blindfolds, implements, an array of sex toys, and even showed her all his favorite websites.

He was the one responsible for really opening her up to anal sex, butt plugs, and one of his favorites, ginger-figging. Jordan enjoyed every minute of introducing her to his world. Similar to Nurse Madison, Jordan really took the time to coach her, and get her to feel comfortable with her own body and sexual desires. There's no doubt that now, Julia is operating totally free, on all cylinders, with absolutely no inhibitions.

Up until now, their wild & kinky adventures had been kept just between each other. Tonight, Jordan was actually expecting a threesome with Julia and Rebecca, especially since they'd all bantered about it for the past several weeks. A part of him was even thinking that a threesome with Julia and Nurse Madison might go down. Now that... is something that he definitely wants to experience.

So to say that Jordan was shocked by this threesome involving Trevor instead of a girl, is an understatement. He was totally caught off guard like a deer in headlights!

However, he can't help but smile inside at the way Julia cleverly pulled this off. The way she planned and directed this male/male/female threesome, and totally sprung it on him, made Jordan realize just how crazy, sexy, kinky, and free-spirited Julia had become.

As Trevor disposed of the condom and cleaned himself up, Julia focused her attention back on Jordan.
"Take me anyway you want, baby!"

Jordan smirked, "You already know that answer."

Julia smiled, opened the drawer of the small table on the side of her bed, and pulled out a tube of lube along with a pretty pink vibrator. She took Jordan's hand and walked him into the living room. She handed him the lube, and then took her position bent over the arm of the sofa. She reached back and spread her own ass cheeks as far as she could, as Jordan greased himself up. The moment Trevor came into the living room, Julia handed him the vibrator.

"I want you to turn this on and hold this to my clit, when I tell you." She directed him, "I'm about to really get my ass reamed!"

Jordan smirked once again, and proceeded to focus on her

amazingly toned, bubble of a butt. He started off gently, and once his dick was fully inside her ass, he started to slowly increase the intensity. After a minute or two, the anal sex felt even better, as Julia concentrated on breathing, and relaxed into it.

"Give it to me, baby!" She called out to Jordan, then immediately squealed as his strong right hand delivered a relentless slap to her right ass cheek.

<SLAP>

He delivered several more intense slaps as he was really fucking her ass hard.
<SLAP><SLAP>
<SLAP>

Julia called out to Trevor, "Now! Hold it right here!"

As Trevor turned on the vibrator, Julia guided his hand to the exact position where she wanted it. She helped hold it in place, firmly pressed against her clit, and teasing her sensitive lady-lips. She let out a number of loud, sexy, moans as Jordan fucked the living daylights out of her tight ass.

"I'm close..." Jordan announced, letting Julia know.

Julia called out to Trevor, "Now! Hold it right here!"

Julia squeezed her ass cheeks as tight as she could, making them clamp onto his penis. Jordan's cock now remained tightly pressed into her rectum, as he exploded and moaned to a climax, "Aah!".

About thirty seconds later, as Jordan's dick was still buried deep in her ass, and Trevor was kissing her, and holding the vibrator to her clit, Julia's body shook like it was in an earthquake and she moaned to an epic orgasm.

"Yes! MMMmmm… God Yes!"

Once things settled down and their orgasms came to an end, Jordan smiled at Julia.

"I'm gonna take a shower babe, and get dressed once again." He laughed, "We still have dinner plans."

"I'll be right in baby," Julia replied, "Let me say goodbye and let Trevor out."

As Jordan retreated to take a shower, Trevor got dressed, and Julia walked him to the door. She gave him a tender, but yet sexy kiss.

"What can I say, Trev?… That was amazing!" She smiled at him.

"It was!" Trevor replied, "but... I was extremely nervous. You, on the other hand, are the sexiest girl on this planet. Jordan is one really lucky guy."

"Well, we aren't actually boyfriend/girlfriend. At least for now." Julia chimed back, "I'm free to date other people and so is he. So call me, Trevor."

"To be honest with you Julia, I would probably get my heart broken with you. I would definitely want you all to myself. I am so into you!" He confesses.

"Awww!" Julia hugs him, "I understand, and it's totally up to you. Besides Jordan, you're the only guy in this school that I would want to date."

Julia then admits, "I'm still finding out a lot about myself, my sexuality, my needs, and my desires."

"I thought you and Rebecca were together... Aren't you with her?" Trevor asked.

"It's the same, we're not exclusive either."

"I'm just curious," Trevor continues, "Why didn't you just have a threesome with her and Jordan?"

"It's simple... I didn't want to be predictable. Plus, I love having a nice, hard penis inside me, and you baby, are super hot! Don't ever doubt yourself."

Julia's words made Trevor's face turn almost as red as her ass cheeks.

"A sexy scenario like that with Rebecca and Jordan might happen in the future, but this was my first threesome... I wanted to make it special." Julia explained, "I'm glad you were a part of it!"

"Well, you already know that it was my first threesome as well... And it was amazing! You are amazing!" Trevor continues, "I wish it could've been with another girl instead of Jordan, but there was no way that I was passing up a chance to fuck you."

Julia laughs at Trevor's last comment as he continues pouring his heart out to her.

"You are stunningly beautiful Julia, inside and out. I'm glad you asked me. This is something I'll remember for the rest of my life!"

"Call me, Trevor," Julia kissed him one last time, "I can show you much more. Trust me, I can really rock your world!"

As Trevor exits her apartment, Julia heads into the shower and joins Jordan. She's worked up quite an appetite and she's really looking forward to further celebrating her birthday with him at her favorite restaurant.

Chapter 4

As they shower together, kiss, and scrub each other down, Julia reminds him, "I can't wait to have more of you after dinner, baby!... This time you're gonna fuck me the old-fashioned way, in my vagina."

Jordan breaks out laughing at her comment, as the warm water massages his back and shoulder blades. He replies back, "Let's not forget that you definitely have an appointment with my leather strap when we get home. I'm really gonna make you dance, after pulling a stunt like that on me!"

Julia smirks and teases him right back, "You have to admit... That was pretty clever of me, wasn't it?"

"Clever for sure!" he responded, "You had me convinced that we were going to have a threesome with Rebecca. I mean... She's been looking me up and down like crazy these past two weeks!"

"First of all... She's been eyeing you up and down because she's dying to fuck you, babe... I tell her just about everything you do to me and how incredible you are... Second of all, Rebecca is similar to me, she hasn't had a lot of sexual partners. I've been taking it slow with her, teaching her some things, showing her some of my toys... The big difference with her is that she's still vanilla. She's still trying to figure out her desires and sexual needs. If I turn you loose on her, you'll ruin her for the rest of her life... you've already ruined me... Hahaha!" Julia erupts with a good laugh, as her hands grab onto his wet, soapy cock.

"You're such a tease! I'm going to strap your ass so hard that you're going to cry a river tonight!"

"I'm counting on it, baby… I've been a really naughty girl." Julia pipes back.

Their sexy banter and their shower together ends and Jordan gets himself together much quicker than Julia does. He heads off to the living room and sits on her sofa, waiting patiently as she continues to get ready. He realizes that after the fuck festival that just went down, Julia now has to re-apply her makeup all over again. Plus, she still needs to get dressed for their dinner date.

This time alone is actually helpful to him as he reflects on so many events that have happened to him so far during his first semester at The Academy. Aside from Julia and the relationship they have, there's also Nurse Madison, and the secret, kinky, adventurous, sex-crazy, affair they share. Then, there's also a harem of other girls, such as Samantha, Cassie, Debbie, Vanessa, and Genna, who all want a piece of him… And let's not forget the flirting that he does with Ms. Jenn as well.

So, even with all this attention, Jordan still can't get Principal Kate off his mind. The way she forced herself on him, and kissed him with so much fire in her office, totally blew his mind. Then when he turned the tables on her and delivered several relentless slaps over her panties, it made him crave her more, if that's even possible.

Add to all this, the fact that he came right out and willingly told her that he has a thing for getting spanked in garages. This, in turn, really seemed to spark her interest. Even though it was just a playful flirt, Jordan made it quite clear to her that she could always discipline him off campus... in her own over-sized garage.

He's already masturbated at least 100 times with the image of her chasing him around the garage with that leather strap clenched tightly in her hand. Once she grabs him, he then pictures her forcefully stripping his clothes off, and delivering that strap so profusely to his bare bottom, that he dances from leg to leg.

That's where his mind has been from the moment he met her on the very first day of his student orientation. Needless to say, along with fucking Principal Kate every which way possible, getting a serious dose of discipline from her, is one fantasy that plays over and over in his mind.

After another 30 minutes or so, Julia came into the living room, ready to go to dinner. She looks beyond stunning in a short black dress that accentuates all her leg muscles and that sexy toned ass of hers. Once Jordan takes a look at her, his smile says it all. He's floored!

"My God, you are beautiful!" he commented.

"Thank you, sweetheart. Ready to go?... I'm starving!" she takes his hand and they exit her apartment.

After a short drive, they arrive and walk in, hand in hand, into the fancy restaurant.

"Hi Thompson, table for two." Jordan announced to the hostess who greeted them.

She leads them to a table overlooking a gorgeous waterfall. The two of them are so stunningly attractive that just about every eye in the room is drawn to them as they walk together. In fact, they pass by another very attractive couple, who are on their way out of the restaurant. That couple also turns their heads to look at them as well.

The man was very handsome, probably in his early-to-mid thirties, and was in great shape. The woman, who is obviously his wife, judging by the size of her diamond ring, is a total knock-out. She looks to be around the same age, mid 30's. Her figure is one that could stop traffic as she's also in phenomenal shape, and totally rocking a tight-fitting red pencil skirt.

Her big brown eyes opened wide, as her wavy, long brown hair swung to one side when she turned her head to take a look at Julia. She wasted no time in complimenting Julia on her sexy, little black dress.

"Oh my God, I love your dress! It looks amazing on you," she tells Julia.

Julia smiles at her, notices her outfit, especially her designer high heels, and politely responds back.
"Thank so much, and I absolutely love your shoes, your skirt,…

and that tattoo is so beautiful!"

Julia was referring to a very pretty tattoo in the shape of an ankh symbol above the woman's left ankle. Actually, what really caught Julia's attention was how spectacular the woman's legs were. They were incredibly toned, but not overly muscular, especially her calf muscles. The stunning woman caught Jordan's eyes as well, but of course, he didn't let on. Just the mere sight of this sophisticated, dark-haired, dark-eyed beauty made him instantly create several hot fantasies in his mind. It's something Jordan usually does, whenever he gets a glimpse of a really attractive woman. Especially, an attractive, older woman, who looks like she would really kick your ass.

Julia also noticed a few other tattoos that also stood out on her. One was a colorful butterfly on the woman's shoulder and another was the third-eye symbol on her forearm. It was obvious this woman was an exercise buff, but Julia also pegged her as someone who was spiritual and had some depth to her. Julia was instantly drawn to these types of tattoos. In fact, she thought they were incredibly sexy, or at least they were sexy on this sensational-looking stranger.

Jordan, and the woman's husband, gave each other a friendly nod as he pulled out the chair for Julia to sit down. The moment they took their seats, Julia commented, "Oh my God, she is so stunning! And those tattoos are so sexy. Maybe I should get one or two on me?"

"Honestly, I love your body the way it is now," Jordan quickly chimed in, "It's perfect with no ink on it."

Once again, Jordan had just the right words to say, as Julia flashed him that sexy smile of hers. Their dinner together at the high-end restaurant came to an end. It was stellar as usual, and their conversation contained everything from sex, spankings, the threesome they just had, to fitness, and even more talk of tattoos.

So far it's been an event-filled night, and it's only 9:30pm. During the entire car ride home, Jordan had been threatening Julia that she was really gonna get it when they got home. His exact words are that she's in for a good, old-fashioned bare bottom strapping. Of course, the sexy birthday girl isn't going to make it easy on him. She fires back, "You got to catch me first!"

"You know I love a good chase," Jordan replied.

"Me too!" Julia smirked and fired back.

They arrive back and just as they are pulling into the school parking lot, Jordan comments.
"I think something is going on here."

"Why? I don't see anything." Julia replied.

Jordan then pointed out, "I'm pretty sure that is an unmarked & undercover police car, and so is that one over there."

Julia's eyes looked at the vehicles that Jordan was pointing to. "Hmmm... Maybe it's another drug arrest?" she commented, "Ms.

Marilyn is serious about ridding this campus of drug use."

"Oh, I know!" Jordan replied.

"Hopefully they arrest Cassie and get her out of my life!" Julia says with a snooty tone.

"Why? Is she doing drugs?"

"I'm just guessing, but think about it." Julia continued, "I know how hard you work out, and I know how much time I put into the gym, and it seems in the last few months that Cassidy's body has made some amazing gains. I mean, she was always pretty. I hate to admit it, but now she looks even better! She obviously gained weight because her butt is bigger. It's actually turned into a nice, round, bubble butt. She never had that... and yet her stomach is much leaner with abs!... And, I hardly ever see her in our gym."

Jordan replied, "She probably works out at another gym off campus."

Julia chimes in, "I don't know... perhaps. But I do know that her dad is a doctor. Maybe he's supplying her with steroids or even other narcotics to sell."

"I don't know, baby... I doubt it. Let's face it, she's not one of your favorite people," Jordan replies.

"Ever since my first year here, we've had many issues with each other. She would constantly switch up the workload and give me all the bullshit farm chores. That's the reason why I got spanked last year by Principal Kate. I was about to knock her lights out." Julia explained.

"Yeah, but that's far from dealing drugs." Jordan recaps.

"So last year, about a week after I got spanked, I saw something. I could swear that I walked in on her giving Amy an injection in the locker room. I'm willing to bet it was Trenbolone, which is a steroid popular for female bodybuilders and athletes."

"Really, babe? Jordan asked.

"Yeah… I mean, I didn't say anything because I didn't want to get into another altercation with her. Especially after getting the first spanking of my life."

Julia went on, "I got there a few seconds too late, and all I saw was Amy rubbing her ass cheek. I did see Cassie throw a vial, along with something else, probably the syringe, into her gym bag, because it made a noise. Then, she stepped in front of it to cover up."

"Okay, so recently, there were a couple more things," Julia continues her rampage and tells him more.

"A few months ago, while I was working late for Nurse Madison, Cassie was in the medical training room. Again, I walked in on her giving another girl a shot in her butt. Cassie played it off and said they were practicing with saline solution. She even joked with me and asked if she could practice on me. Of course, I told her to get lost. The interesting thing is, the saline solution that was in that room, still had the tamper-proof wrapping around the cap. It was never even opened!"

"You sure about that?" Jordan questioned.

"I sure am! Then, just a couple days ago, I saw her downtown at the coffee shop with another girl who isn't from our school… She gave the girl a gift-wrapped present, which is no big deal, but the girl never opened it. I mean, if it was your birthday and a friend met you at a coffee shop and gave you a present, you would open it… Wouldn't you? To make matters worse, on the way out I saw the girl hand Cassie an envelope as she hugged her. I don't know, Jordan. It might be all hearsay, but I don't trust her."

Julia then breaks it up by interjecting some of her quirky humor. She turns her focus to Jordan and jokes, "Let's hope these cops aren't here to arrest you. I promise, I didn't say a thing about your gun to anyone."

Jordan quickly responded, "I told you. I have that for protection only. It's a crazy world out there, especially on school campuses."

"It's okay, babe. I promise I'll visit you if they lock you up." Julia jokes.

"Geez thanks!" Jordan rolled his eyes at her.

Julia smirks at him, "I know, I know… I'm really gonna get it.

Just give me a few seconds to kickoff these heels and run once we get inside."

She then leans over and gives Jordan a super sexy, super passionate kiss, followed by a good firm grip of her right hand over the front of his black pants.

"Mmm… Hard again, huh? Thinking about me, babe?" Julia teased.

"Yep! I'm thinking how fun it's going to be for me to put some red stripes across your pretty ass!" He chuckled.

Both of them laugh in unison at the silly flirtatious humor they have as they get out of the car and walk towards her apartment. She takes out her keys and right before she goes to unlock the door, her phone rings. She looks at the screen display.

"It's my mom." She tells Jordan as she answers her phone.

"Hi mom! Thank you for my birthday gift. I love it!" She continues, "Yes, I had an amazing birthday. Jordan just took me out to dinner and we're just getting home now. Hold on, mom."

Julia starts to prepare for their fun spanking adventure as she kicks her high-heeled shoes off, and sends Jordan a sexy wink. She then handed him the keys to open the door to her apartment, "Damn, I forgot to leave the lights on. The light switch is on the right-hand side."

She smiles with all that sex appeal once again at Jordan, and continues talking to her mom, "Okay mom. Sure... lunch tomorrow... What time and where?"

As Julia coordinates the final details for lunch with her mom tomorrow, Jordan puts the key in the door to her apartment. He's definitely looking forward to chasing her down and having some play time alone with her. He opens the door and fumbles for the light switch on the wall. Out of nowhere, his arm is forcefully grabbed, and he's pushed against the wall of her apartment.

"That's him!" is shouted from a female voice across the room.

The next voice Jordan heard was that of a police officer reading him his rights.
"Jordan Thompson, you are under arrest. Hands behind your back."
"You have the right to remain silent, anything you say can and will be used against you..."

Chapter 5

"What am I being arrested for?" Jordan yelled out, as he felt the officer push him into the wall.

The room was still completely dark since he was unable to turn the light switch on before all this went down. It happened all so fast that Jordan totally lost his bearings. The next thing he felt was the cold metal handcuff getting clamped tightly around his right wrist. Jordan's left arm was still pinned behind his back by the officer, who was using a fair amount of force on him.

"I have rights… What are you arresting me for?" Jordan asked again, as the officer proceeded and clamped the handcuff around his left wrist.

He was now fully secured with his arms cuffed tightly behind his back. His face was pushed hard against the wall of Julia's pitched-black living room until the officer forcefully spun him 180 degrees. Jordan felt a more than firm push on his chest that made the back of his shoulders slam hard against the wall.

"Put on the lights, Ma'am," the officer called out to Julia. "And make sure your hands stay where I can see them."

"Yes, officer," Julia replied, as she flicked the switch and illuminated her living room.

In a heartbeat, Julia's living room was filled with light as Jordan's eyes now came face to face with the arresting officer.

"You are being arrested for being too fucking sexy!" The officer sternly announced.

To Jordan's surprise, it was the stunningly beautiful woman they had just run into at the restaurant. She was now decked out in a full Kentville Police uniform. His eyes then glanced across the room to see Rebecca and Julia standing together giggling like two preschool girls.

"This is officer Eden Monroe," Julia announced, "Not only is she as hot as fuck, and one strong, bad-ass woman, she really is a Kentville cop!"

"Holy shit!… You scared the FUCK out of me, baby," Jordan replied.

Julia smirked and continued, "Since you just allowed me to have my threesome with you and Trevor, I felt it was only fair that to allow you to have the same with me and Rebecca. You might also get some extra bonuses from Officer Monroe… I'll leave that up to her since she's married as has some limitations."

"I can't believe that you rigged this all up," Jordan smirked at her.

"She sure did!" Eden replied. "You are one lucky boy to have such a sexy and creative girlfriend!"

"And the good news is…" Eden continued, "She gave me her complete permission to do anything I want to you!"

"So then what are your limitations?" Jordan asked, a bit confused.

"I can't fuck you," Eden continued to explain.

"That was my husband, Zach, that you saw in the restaurant. We have an open marriage, but we will only do full-on intercourse if we are both in the room. Unless we have agreed and talked about it in advance. That's what our limits are. Everything else is totally allowed!"

The stunning officer immediately pushed herself into his body while rubbing her hand up and down the front of his black dress pants. She proceeded to give Jordan a kiss that was so hot and sexy that it almost made him melt right there against the wall. The minute her tongue left his mouth, Rebecca came running over.

"My turn!" Rebecca announced. "I've been waiting for this!"

The moment Eden took a step backward, Rebecca wasted no time and plunged her tongue fully into his mouth. She totally lost herself as their kiss went on for what seemed to be an eternity.

"Fuck!... You are so H-O-T!" she announced, and finally pulled away from his lips.

"Told ya' he's an amazing kisser!" Julia smirked as she now approached him.

She then stepped forward and made her talented tongue deliver a kiss that was not only filled with passion, it was also gift-wrapped with an abundance of love.

"I love you so much, baby," Julia whispered into his right ear and then playfully nibbled his earlobe.

Eden now stepped forward, and once again, her right hand started rubbing over the front of his pants to fondle his dick. She actually pulled Jordan away from the wall so that her left hand could get a good squeeze of his ass cheeks.

"Mmm… I can't wait to get at this body!" she smirked.

Eden then walked in front of him, stared into his emerald green eyes, and gave a gentle rub over his testicles.

"Let's get you nice and hard again, you sexy-boy," she smirked as her hands fondled him.

The mature and beyond stunning woman gave him another kiss that was even hotter than her first one. Her full, super-plush red lips totally engulfed his entire mouth as her tongue made sure to taste every morsel. She even slid her tongue across the front of his teeth, then gave a sexy little bite to his lower lip, before she traced it down the side of his neck. This time her entire mouth covered his right ear as her voice whispered in a low and incredibly sexy tone.

"I am going to spank your ass so hard with my leather strap that you'll be dancing like crazy."

Her big brown eyes looked right into his and that pretty face of hers had that get-down-to-business, seriously stern look that made him just flip-out. That's about all it took, and once again, Jordan's body quickly reacted and his cock returned to a full-on erection.

"MMM... That's more like it," Eden whispered to him as her hand felt his dick grow and continued to rub it over his dress pants. "It's obvious that you like hearing me talk dirty and telling you just how I'm going to handle you."

She walked around him in a half-circle and now whispered into his other ear.

"I can't wait to get at that ass of yours, young man."

These sexy whispers going through his ears and penetrating his brain were working wonders and getting him turned-on like crazy. Eden continued to feel every inch of him grow as her hand gently rubbed up and down over the front of his pants.

"I'm going to strip you down to your birthday suite, Jordan Thompson!" her soft raspy voice whispered, "And I'm gonna spank you right in front of your girlfriend and Rebecca."

Once again, Eden teased him and walked back over to his other ear. She then followed it up with another sexy whisper.

"Don't worry baby, I'm going to let you get your revenge on them. I want to watch you fuck them senseless!"

Eden walked right back in front of him, and held his handsome face as she planted another erotic kiss that made his knees completely buckle. Those kisses and her entire vibe was steaming with a sex appeal that literally made his dick throb.

Julia and Rebecca were watching every move and enjoying the way Eden was taking control of Jordan. They sat right next to each other on the sofa as their hands touched and fondled each other. Rebecca didn't waste anytime and had her hand buried so far underneath Julia's pretty black dress rubbing her vagina, that it almost made Julia orgasm.

Eden remained face to face right in front of Jordan as she stared into his big green eyes. She had that very stern and somewhat mean look in her pretty brown eyes that was a huge turn-on to him. It made him instantly reflect on several of the older women in his past that had spanked him. As images of those sexy women and all the past spankings they gave him filled his head, he felt another amazing sensation. Eden's hands wandered down to rub his testicles, then proceeded to apply a more than firm grip to them. It didn't matter that he still had his pants on, the way she cupped his testicles and squeezed using this amount of force, made him gasp for air.

"Mmm… good boy," Eden responded in a very sexy voice, as she watched him take a deep breath. "There's plenty more where this came from."

She gave his balls one last squeeze before she stepped away from him and signaled to Julia.

"Julia, get the rope out of my bag," she called over as she displayed a super-cute, but devilish grin on her pretty face.

As Jordan remained handcuffed with his arms behind his back, Eden quickly unfastened his belt. She then tugged his pants down to his ankles and proceeded to remove his shoes and socks. After she tossed those items aside, she slid his pants off his body, before tossing them to join the other clothing items of his on the floor.

She then unbuttoned his stylish dress shirt and once again, spun him around 180 degrees so that his face was back to being pressed into the wall. This time, she unfastened the handcuffs just long enough to take his shirt off his body, before spinning him back around to face her. Eden then cuffed his hands in front of his body as she fastened the long rope to them.

She led him into the center of Julia's living room and threw one end of the rope over the thick wooden exposed beam of Julia's vaulted ceiling. She gave the end of the rope to Julia and instructed her.

"Pull it tight and tie it to the legs of your table."

Within a matter of seconds, Jordan's arms were stretched upward over his head as Julia secured the rope to her furniture.

"MMM... Mmm... Mmm...," Eden mumbled as she walked in a

circle around Jordan.

She then reached into her bag, retrieved a thick leather strap, and clenched it tightly in her right hand. The strap was very similar to one that's used here at the Academy. It had the same well-crafted, glossy wooden handle, with a small rope that went around the wrist. The strap itself was a faded brown leather color that made it clear it had plenty of wear. The only difference this strap had to the one used at the school was that it had several matching holes drilled into each side. Eden gave another devilish smirk as she held the strap up to Jordan's face. She continued to tease and threaten him in her sexy kind of way.

"Oh Yes, my dear," Eden called out, "Rumor has it that you love everything about spanking... And Julia filled me in on how you always tan her pretty little ass."

Eden continued as she positioned herself behind him.

"Tonight, you're the one that's going to get his ass tanned!"

Jordan turned his head to look over his left shoulder. He was now about as hard as a tree with his cock pointing so far upwards towards the ceiling that it made his thin, gray and black striped athletic underwear look like a pup-tent.

"Look at this beautiful specimen!" Eden announced as she circled him again, allowing her fingers to trace his broad shoulders and muscular chest, before proceeding down to his chiseled abs.

"I'm looking!" Rebecca quickly chimed with her eyes opened as wide as can be. "Oh my God his dick! It's about to bust through his underwear. I can't wait to fuck his brains out!"

"Chill-out Bec," Julia chuckled and replied, "He's going to pound you into oblivion once I give him the go ahead."

"And I can't wait to see that," Eden announced in an incredibly sexy voice, "But first, I'm going to take my strap to his tight ass and make him dance!"

She then stepped behind him, slid her fingers inside the waistband of his underwear, and gave them an assertive tug.

Chapter 6

"Mmmm… Hmmm… A-B-S-O-L-U-T-E-L-Y lovely!" Eden emphasized and smiled from ear to ear as she focused on Jordan's amazingly tight, round ass.

Again, she paced around him in a circle to make sure she took in the sight of his totally erect dick, as well as his super-cute, muscular ass.

"His body is even more beautiful than you described, Julia," Eden called out as her eyes took in the full view of Jordan's completely naked body.

Eden then spun him around to make sure that Rebecca and Julia got a full view of his sexy body as well.

"F-U-C-K... He is so HOT!" Rebecca immediately smirked. "You are one lucky girl, Jul, to have that dick fuck you all the time."

Julia smiled at her kinky best friend with benefits, then followed it up with a kiss, as she and Rebecca continued to fondle each other on the sofa.

"Do you know what I love the most about spanking?" Eden asked Jordan in a very seductive yet stern kind of voice.

"No Ma'am," Jordan replied as he turned his head to look over his left shoulder at her.

Jordan, who's definitely had his share of beautiful and sexy women, couldn't help but silently smile as he looked back at Eden. She was about as beautiful and as sexy as a woman could be. Her long dark hair, big brown eyes, with an absolutely stunning smile to compliment her curvy, well-toned body, has his dick throbbing.

She planted another kiss on him and whispered in a sexy, low voice, "What I like about spanking is…."

"E-V-E-R-Y …. FUCKING…. THING!" Eden loudly replied in a sarcastically stern voice.

Jordan felt her left hand take hold of his upward stretched left bicep. The next thing he heard was the faint whistling sound of the strap cutting through the air as she swung it with serious intensity.

<CRACK>

That merciless swat landed a bit more on Jordan's right ass cheek and immediately painted a thick red stripe across it.

"UMM..." Jordan mumbled through this gritted-teeth, trying not to give her the satisfaction of hearing him yelp.

Eden smirked as her eyes took in the sight of the new freshly painted stripe across his ass. She kept a firm grip on his left arm and swung again with even more force.

<WHACK>

The strap landed dead in the center of Jordan's rear-end, creating another thick, bright red stripe.

"Aahh!" he made a small, slightly yelping sound as his right foot came off the floor.

"Trying to hold it in, huh, honey?" Eden smirked. "We'll see how long that lasts."

She raised the strap high and delivered three vicious swats one after another that totally made him change his tune.

<WHACK><CRACK><CRACK>

"OOW!… OOH!" he now clearly responded, as his left foot, then his right foot alternated and came off the floor.

"Make him dance, Eden!" Julia called out. "He always loves watching me bounce up and down when he straps my ass. Now it's his turn!"

Eden sent a diabolical smile back to Julia as her left hand now grabbed a fist full of his hair.

"No worries, babe," Eden replied to Julia, "I promise you… I will make him dance!"

<CRACK> <CRACK><WHACK><CRACK>

Her spanks with that strap were unforgiving and Jordan naturally responded by dancing from leg to leg, as well as tucking his body inward.

"STICK THAT ASS OUT!" Eden scolded him as her left hand traveled down and took hold of his testicles.

She gave his tight, perfectly shaped, balls a good hard squeeze, then continued to cup them in the palm of her hand and swung the strap again with everything she had.

<WHACK><WHACK><CRACK>
<CRACK><WHACK>

"OOOW!... OUCH!"

Jordan's ass was completely on fire as he felt the full effect of this relentless strapping from the sexy, older woman. Eden was absolutely right. Totally tied up with his arms extended upward over his head, all Jordan could do was dance... And that he did, very well!

Eden loved every minute of making him yelp, hop up and down, and dance like a champion as she delivered her thick leather strap to his bare bottom. The deep red and purple stripes now overlapped each other in various directions as Jordan's tight, round ass became even more plump and swollen.

Rebecca and Julia's eyes got to see a show that would never

forget as Jordan couldn't help but try to spin around and dance away from this severe strapping. His huge dick continued to point straight up towards the ceiling and looked like a POGO stick as he hopped in place from the way Eden was going to town on his ass.

As much as her spanking hurt, it also had him turned-on beyond belief. He loved being man-handled by a strong, sophisticated, and absolutely stunning-looking woman. Not to mention, the way Eden's hand was squeezing his balls and that stern, yet incredibly sexy look on her face really added to his excitement. And let's not forget the way she looked in that police uniform. All this, plus being the only one naked in the room and having Julia and Rebecca's eyes glued to him as his ass was getting profusely strapped, totally fulfilled the exhibitionist side of him.

Eden paused for a moment and stepped back to take in the sight of her work. Jordan's ass looked even sexier to her as they were totally marked up and perfectly swollen. She smiled even more when Julia called out.

"His ass looks even more bubbly right now!"

This also prompted Eden to give a quick reply, "Oh, I'm far from done with his ass!"

She then paced in front of him and feasted her eyes on his amazing, rock-hard dick. She dropped her strap for a moment as her right hand started to stroke the shaft of his cock. Jordan tilted his head backwards as he felt the heavenly way she was stroking him.

Eden took it a step further, and immediately dropped to her knees. She made sure Julia and Rebecca had a nice view as her entire mouth engulfed his dick.

"MMMmmm!" Jordan's moans were now completely pleasure-filled as Eden proceeded to give him a phenomenal, world-class blow job.

She traced her tongue up and down, licking every inch of his massive cock along with his testicles. She then spun him around, grabbed hold of his totally sore ass, and pulled his cheeks as far apart as possible. Jordan quickly responded with a loud sexy moan as Eden really dug her nails into his tender cheeks. Eden proceeded to really tease him as she gave Jordan several delicate licks across all the maroon-colored marks on his ass cheeks. She made sure her tongue traced his entire bare bottom and didn't miss a bruise or mark. Then, she even used her mouth to blow some cool air onto his rear-end to give him an additional sensation and to contrast all the heat coming from his skin.

Jordan was now totally lost in the way her tongue felt as she licked and then blew cool air over every inch of his bare bottom. Once Eden was satisfied that she didn't miss a spot, she dug her fingernails even harder into his ass cheeks to hold them tightly. She then pulled and spread them apart as wide as she possibly could while she flattened out her talented tongue and licked his asshole.

"Whhhhoooa!… Mmmm!"

Jordan immediately responded and really began to pant as Eden's tongue now penetrated his rectum. She continued to hold his ass cheeks far apart as he squirmed in place with excitement.

"Ahh!"

His body was now slightly quivering from being turned-on so much. To say that Jordan's dick was as hard as a rock right now would be an understatement. His dick was so thick and so erect that it almost touched the ceiling. Of course, this made Rebecca and Julia crave it even more.

"God, I want to suck his dick," Rebecca chimed. "Look at the size of it!"

"He always gets that hard when I finger and rim him," Julia called out in confirmation. "He really flips out over ass play!"

"He's not the only one that loves a good rimming and some ass play," Rebecca quickly commented to Julia. "I love it when you do that to me!"

After spending what seemed to be an eternity, thoroughly licking every inch of his asshole inside and out, and driving him completely crazy, Eden paused for a moment and signaled the girls to come over. She reached into her bag and pulled out a blindfold. As Jordan remained in the center of the room with his arms tied upward, she slipped the blindfold over his eyes and announced.

"We're gonna play a little game!"

Chapter 7

"I want you to tell us who's kissing you," Eden announced.

She waited for about 10 seconds and made sure that Julia and Rebecca stayed silent before she proceeded. Jordan then felt the sexy sensation of a tongue licking his lower back and proceeding all the way up his spine, before stopping just shy of his neck.

"Whose tongue was that?" Eden asked him.

Completely blindfolded and not having the sense of sight, Jordan flat-out guessed.

"Umm… Julia's," he replied.

<SLAP>

Eden delivered a vicious hand slap to his bare ass.

"Ouch!" he yelped.

"WRONG!" she responded. "That was me!"

"Stick out your tongue," she instructed him. "And flatten it out."

Jordan followed her orders and stuck his tongue out as he flattened it to his bottom lip. He then felt another tongue glide over his in an extremely sexy way.

"Who was that?" Eden asked him.

"That was definitely Julia," Jordan replied with confidence.

"Right you are!" Eden replied, but delivered another intense hand slap that once again made his feet come off the ground.

<SLAP>

"Hey, I got that right!" Jordan responded. "Why did you spank me?"

"My game, my rules," Eden giggled.

She gave another hand signal and within a couple of seconds, Jordan was moaning with pleasure and feeling on cloud nine. His head titled back again as his huge dick was being thoroughly licked in every direction. After a minute or so, Eden put a stop to the action and asked again.

"Whose tongue was that?"

"That was yours," Jordan replied.

"Hmmm… You're getting good at this game," she commented with a smirk.

After hearing the snap of a finger, Jordan suddenly felt another tongue lick up and down the shaft of his cock, before it turned into an all-out blow job. At the same time, another tongue rimmed his asshole, while a third tongue kissed his ear, then traced down his face and tasted his tongue.

Jordan was now moaning loudly in between labored breathing.

"Oh my God! This feels amazing!" he announced, as his mind was getting completely blown to smithereens.

After another minute or so, and with the sound of another finger snap, all the action stopped. Eden waited a bit before asking.

"Name the tongues," she asked him with a cute giggle in her voice.

Jordan responded with confidence, "Julia was definitely blowing me... You were the one kissing me, and Rebecca was rimming me."

The girls giggled in unison as Eden delivered another slap to his ass.

<SLAP>

"Right again!" she called out.

She then removed the blindfold from his eyes and gave him another sexy and passionate kiss. Eden was also turned-on beyond belief as she stepped away and motioned for Julia to kiss him. After totally kissing him with every ounce of passion she had, Julia pulled Rebecca over.

"Kiss him the way you kiss me," Julia coached her friend. "And make sure you squeeze his balls. He loves that!"

Rebecca smiled, as she placed her left hand on his chiseled jaw line, and cupped his tight testicles in her right hand. She gave them a nice squeeze that made Jordan gasp, while she planted a very sensual and erotic kiss on him. Even though Jordan remained handcuffed and tied, it didn't affect the talent of his tongue, and the way he kissed her back. He kissed Rebecca with so much fire that it literally blew her skirt up!

"Yummy!" she quickly commented after kissing him. "You were right, Jul… He's pure fire!"

Eden smiled at Rebecca, and also comment to Julia, "He sure is!… I'm so fucking wet right now... All I want to do is fuck your boyfriend!"

"Well, I won't tell your husband," Julia smiled at her. "I would love to watch you fuck him."

Julia followed up with, "And for the record, Jordan's technically not my boyfriend. None of us here are in an exclusive relationship. We are way too young and we need to focus on our studies. We're just trying to relieve some stress and get through this incredibly hard and demanding school. So please, by all means, fuck his brains out and let Rebecca and I watch!"

Eden laughed, "I would love to, but I can't. I have to honor the agreement my husband and I made with each other."

Eden then smirked as an idea came into her head.

"However, I would do a trade. I'll fuck Jordan and you can fuck my husband."

"Your husband is totally hot!" Julia replied, "I'm down for that!"

"My husband's eyes just about popped out of their sockets when he saw you in the restaurant," Eden chuckled. "He always had a thing for red-heads."

Rebecca quickly interrupted, "Hey!... I want in on this action!... Don't leave me out!"

Eden laughed, "That's a deal. My husband would totally flip-out to have a threesome with you and Julia. He'll be in heaven with a cute little blonde like you added to the mix."

"What do you say, handsome?" Eden now smiled at Jordan in her sexy, sophisticated kind of way. "I heard how great of a spanker you are, so you can get your revenge on me. Then you can fuck my brains out... Anyway you want!"

"Are you sure you're ready for that?" Jordan teased back in a cocky tone. "I might ruin you. You may never want your husband again."

Eden laughed at Jordan's quirky humor as she moved in closer and removed the handcuffs. The moment his hands became free, he rubbed his tender ass in attempt to ease the soreness.

"Oh, no you don't!" Eden sarcastically pulled his hands away. "I'm still in charge tonight… You're getting one last round of spankings, from each of us… Then you're gonna give me and Julia an amazing show as we watch you fuck the daylights out of Rebecca!"

"Oh my God!" Rebecca replied, in a panting voice, "I'm so wet and turned-on right now, that I'm doing everything I can not to play with myself."

"Wait until he pounds the hell out of you," Julia smirked at her cute friend. "Trust me, you are going to be in heaven when you feel that beautiful dick of his inside of you. I promise… It will be worth the wait."

Eden now pulled a high back chair from the dining room table into the center of the living room. She took hold of Jordan's wrist and pulled him over the back of the chair, forcing him to bend over.

"Go pick your implement, Julia," she instructed. "Give him 4 of your best."

Julia smiled as she retrieved a wooden paddle from Eden's kinky toy bag.

"Perfect!" Eden called out to her in approval as she held Jordan firmly in place over the chair. "Paddle his ass… And don't hold back!"

Chapter 8

Eden tightened her grip on Jordan's wrists as she held him over the back of the high-back wooden chair. Her cute smirk turned into a full-on smile as she watched Julia take aim and tap the wooden paddle several times on Jordan's ass. Julia placed her left hand on the lower portion of Jordan's back as she delivered her first of four intense swats.

<CRACK>

"Ooow!" Jordan immediately yelped as his feet shuffled in place.

"That was 1," Eden announced.

Without waiting too long, Julia took aim again and delivered. This one landed perfectly on the upper thighs and lower, sit-spot region of Jordan's already bruised bottom.

<WHACK>

"Uh!" Jordan managed to contain the pain through his gritted teeth.

"Give him 2 more… Hard!" Eden smiled at Julia.

"This is payback, baby," Julia chuckled as she took aim on Jordan's cute ass.

<CRACK><CRACK>

She delivered her last two in succession with no pause between them. Those swats really made Jordan squirm and dance over the chair as he yelped loudly.

"OOOW!"

"Good job, babe," Eden sent her pretty smile over to Julia.

Julia replied with a chuckle, "Yeah, but I know I'm in for it when he gets a hold of my ass."

"He's going to have to wait because I can't wait to get my hands on you," Eden smirked, as her eyes gave Julia's tight little athletic body a thorough and sexy look up and down.

"Your turn, Rebecca," Eden called out, "Pick an implement and spank him."

Rebecca giggled like a child looking through a toy store as she fumbled through several items in Eden's toy bag.

"I'll use this on him," she announced as she held up a thin black riding crop.

"Careful, Bec," Julia laughed as she warned her, "You've never got a spanking from Jordan before, so it's only a matter of time until he gets his revenge on you and tans your cute cheeks."

Rebecca's eyes glistened as she focused on Jordan's amazing ass.

She stood slightly off to the left side of him as Eden continued to hold him over the chair. Of course, Rebecca was more than primed and dying to feel his dick inside of her. She couldn't help but let her left hand grab hold of the shaft of his cock and give him a few strokes.

"God, I'm dying for this!" she announced as her hand then moved down to squeeze his testicles.

Jordan turned his head to the left and took in sight of Rebecca's adorable face as she continued to fondle him.

"I'm going to fuck the hell out of you, little girl!" Jordan replied with a more than cocky tone.

"Spank him!" Eden instructed her. "Hard and fast!"

Rebecca held onto his totally erect cock in her left hand as she raised the crop high. For someone that wasn't too familiar with giving a spanking, she did more than wonderful as she delivered four incredibly hard swats, one after another with the riding crop. The sound of the crop whistled through the air and then made a high-pitched sound as it connected to Jordan's bare bottom.

<CRACK><SMACK><CRACK><CRACK>

"Yeoow!"

Jordan immediately responded, and once again, his legs danced off the ground as Eden held him in place.

"Very impressive, Rebecca," Eden smirked as she let go of Jordan and watched him do a little spanking dance.

"Uummm… Cute!" she smiled as her eyes watched him bounce up and down and rub his bottom.

She then signaled for Rebecca and Julia to come over to her. As soon as Rebecca was within reach, Eden lifted her cute dress upwards and totally removed it from her body. She didn't stop there as she unfastened her bra, and tossed it down on the living room carpet.

Without wasting another second, Eden's hands slid inside Rebecca's pretty white-laced panties and tugged them down to her ankles. She instructed Rebecca to step out of them, and once she was completely naked, Eden spun her around to get a full look at her young athletic body.

"You are absolutely adorable," she called out, as her big brown eyes took in the sight of Rebecca's tight little body.

She slid her tongue over Rebecca's small but very perky breasts, before stopping and applying a gentle suction to her strawberry nipples.

"MMMmm!" Rebecca quickly responded as Eden's finger also traveled down and rubbed her wet pussy.

"Someone is incredibly wet," she smirked as her index and

middle finger plunged into Rebecca's vagina.

"OOO!… Yes!" Rebecca immediately moaned as she felt Eden's pretty long fingers explore every inch of her pussy.

"Breathe deep, in and out," Eden coached her, and continued to finger her.

"Oooh!… Mmmm!"

Rebecca let out some pleasure-filled moans and squirmed in place as the sexy, sophisticated older woman fingered the hell out of her. Eden smirked as she looked over at Jordan and announced, "Don't worry, baby… You'll be getting at her soon. I'm just making sure she's nice and wet for you!"

Eden then dropped to her knees and started gently licking Rebecca's clitoris. She dug her long nails into Rebecca's cute little ass to give her a dose of pain to go along with the pleasure.

"Ooouch!…. Mmmm!… Oh my God!" Rebecca instantly responded.

Eden grabbed her hand and led her over to the plush, well-cushioned sofa. She guided Rebecca into a seated position, and continued to lick every inch of her young vagina. Her experienced tongue danced all over Rebecca's clit as her fingers, once again, plunged deep into her vagina.

"God! Yes!" Rebecca moaned in an out of breath voice. "I'm

getting close."

"Take a deep breath, Rebecca," Eden coached her and quickly stopped everything that she was doing.

She signaled to Jordan, who was standing next to Julia, watching all the hot action. Once Jordan came within reach, Eden wrapped her lips around his huge cock and started blowing him. She made sure Jordan was as hard as possible as his dick pointed straight up towards the ceiling.

"You ready to fuck her senseless?" Eden asked him.

"Hell yeah!" Jordan replied with zero hesitation.

Eden reached into the front pocket of her uniform and pulled out a condom. She opened it up, slid it over Jordan's totally erect dick, and announced with a devilish smirk on her face.

"I need to do one more thing to her before you fuck her brains out."

Chapter 9

Eden quickly took a seat on the sofa and assertively yanked Rebecca over her knee.

"I need to redden this pretty little ass of hers!" she called out as she raised her hand high in the air and unleashed a series of hard and fast slaps.

<SLAP><SLAP><SLAP><SLAP>
<SLAP><SLAP><SLAP>

"Oow!... Ouch!"

Those slaps instantly made Rebecca yelp in pain as her pretty round cheeks turned as red as an apple.

<SLAP><SLAP><SLAP>
<SLAP>

"Ooow"

Jordan and Julia smiled from ear to ear as they watched Eden, looking as sexy as can be, and still completely dressed in her police uniform, give Rebecca a serious over the knee spanking. Rebecca's cute toned legs were now kicking up and down as Eden really laid into her.

<SLAP><SLAP>
<SLAP><SLAP><SLAP>

"YEEEOW!… OOO!"

Rebecca squirmed and did one final dance all over Eden's lap, before the spanking came to an end.

"THERE!" Eden sardonically called out. "Now she's ready for good fuck!"

She gave Jordan a "go-ahead" nod of her head as she got up from the sofa and pulled Julia onto an over-sized chair to watch.

Jordan wasted no time as he flipped Rebecca onto her back. He couldn't resist tasting her first as his tongue went straight to licking her pussy. Rebecca's mind was totally blown as she went from feeling the pain of Eden's spanking, right back to feeling total pleasure as Jordan's tongue licked her like an ice cream cone.

"Oh my God!… Yes!… Fuck me, Jordan!" she called out, in an out of breath voice. "I want your dick inside me."

Jordan smiled as he pulled her down off the sofa and onto the carpet. He then maneuvered himself on top of her as she wrapped her legs around his hips. Her pussy was as wet as a flowing stream and Jordan gave a full, forceful thrust of his hips that made her squeal in delight.

"OOOhhh! YES!" Rebecca instantly responded as his totally erect cock penetrated her pussy.

Julia, who was now sitting on Eden's lap, couldn't help but call out.

"Give us a show, baby… Pound her just like you pound me!"

Eden and Julia's eyes got the treat of their life as they watched Jordan's cute red ass vigorously bounce up and down like a basketball as he began fucking the daylights out of Rebecca. In a matter of seconds, he was pounding her with the force of a jack hammer as the sound of his hips slamming against her tight little body filled the living room.

"OOOOO!… Mmmm!" Rebecca's moans increased in volume as Jordan's dick did a number on her.

He was ramming her pussy so hard that she just about felt his dick in her throat. Her breathing was so labored that she could hardly even moan. Julia remained sitting on Eden's lap as they both reveled in having ring-side-seats to the live sex show between these two super-hot bodies.

"Harder, baby!" Julia called out to Jordan, knowing just how incredible he was at fucking.

Jordan obliged as he kicked it up a notch and really rammed the hell out of Rebecca. Her pussy was in heaven from the way his dick felt, and she quickly announced.

"Ahh! Yes!… I'm close!"

Jordan was far from done with her as he quickly stopped fucking her and pulled his dick out of her pussy. He helped her up from the carpet, only to bend her cute body over the arm of the over-sized sofa. He looked down at her amazingly tight red ass, that was covered with Eden's hand-prints all over it like it was a piece of fresh meat.

He then turned and looked over at Julia with a smirk on his face as he pushed his dick right back inside of Rebecca's soaking wet pussy. Once again, his hips were thrusting with full force and the sound of his body slamming against hers filled the room. Jordan didn't stop there. While he continued to fuck her bent over the sofa with everything he had, he raised his right hand high, and delivered a flurry of relentless slaps to her ass.

<SLAP><SLAP><SLAP><SLAP><SLAP
<SLAP><SLAP>

"OOOW!… Ouch!.. God Yes!... I'm coming!" Rebecca screamed out.

Jordan gave her one last series of slaps, before he forcefully plunged his index finger deep into her asshole.

"AAHHH!… YES!… Oh My God!… Oh My G-O-D!" Rebecca moaned into an orgasm as her entire body shook like a leaf in a windstorm.

Jordan gave a few more deep, hard thrusts and then held his cock deep inside of her. His own sexy moans filled the room and accompanied hers as they both experienced pure ecstasy. It took a few minutes for them both to return down to earth. Once they did, Rebecca embraced him and gave him another super-sexy, long, passionate kiss.

"That was amazing!" she complimented him.

"Ditto," Jordan smiled at her, as he hugged her tight.

Rebecca now flashed Julia a cute smile. "And I have you to thank for all this. You set all this up! God, I love you, babe."

"Haha!" Julia smiled, as she made a heart symbol out of her hands, and giggled back, "Luv U too, Bec. You have no idea how sexy you both looked. God, I wish I caught it on video."

"Maybe next time," Rebecca giggled as she walked over to Eden.

She gave Eden a soft, beautiful kiss on her lips, and commented.

"You are one fierce and sexy woman, Officer Eden Monroe. You can arrest me anytime!"

"This is just the start. I plan on having a lot more adventures with you and Julia," Eden smirked back at her, "And I can't wait to see you with my husband."

"I need a shower," Jordan interrupted with a slight chuckle.

"I'm joining you," Rebecca quickly added.

"Great!… I get to have this hottie all to myself," Eden chimed as her hand slipped underneath the V-neck of Julia's pretty black dress.

She delicately rubbed and fondled Julia's perky breasts over her pretty bra, before giving them a little harder squeeze. Then, she looked at Rebecca and Jordan and announced in her slightly raspy voice.

"You might want to hurry back. It's our turn to give you both a show!"

With Julia sitting upright on her lap, Eden traced her tongue in a delightfully sexy way down the side of Julia's pretty neck and all over the front of her upper shoulders. Jordan's eyes just about popped out of their sockets, and he couldn't help but comment.

"Okay!… We'll make it fast. I don't want to miss a moment of watching you and Julia."

He quickly took hold of Rebecca's hand and started walking towards the bathroom. As Jordan and Rebecca disappeared into the bathroom for their shower, Eden now turned all her attention to Julia.

"I R-E-A-L-L-Y can't wait to get at Y-O-U!" she emphasized.

Julia loved hearing this and immediately smiled down at Eden.

She opened her mouth wide to take in another dose of Eden's super-talented tongue. They both shared a kiss so hot and steamy that it belonged in a blockbuster movie. Eden and Julia continued kissing each other for what seemed to be an eternity before finally coming up for air.

"God, you are so beautiful," Julia complimented Eden. "And so sexy!"

"And you drive me crazy," Eden replied. "This little body of yours is perfection!"

Eden flashed her a smile so bright that it could rival the sun as she pulled Julia to her feet. She then spun her around and unzipped the back of Julia's sexy black dress before tugging it downward and completely off her body. She immediately gave Julia several playful pats on her cute little bubble ass and announced.

"I can't wait to put you over my knee."

Julia, standing with just her black panties and matching bra, smiled and immediately spun around. Once again, she embraced Eden with another kiss so hot that it could've erupted the entire building.

"Now that's a talented little tongue," Eden complimented her once the kiss ended.

"You can do whatever you want to me, but I can't wait to lick your pussy," Julia chimed back in a whispered voice.

"Ditto!" Eden replied as she tugged Julia's panties off and flung them on the carpet.

She then unfastened Julia's bra and pulled it off her body. Eden's eyes glistened like stars in the night as she took in the sight of Julia's totally naked, perfectly petite body. She couldn't help but comment on the state of her red ass, totally covered with handprints all over it.

"Looks like Jordan already spanked you tonight," Eden chuckled.

"He did," Julia replied with her own sexy giggle, "But… after all…."

She then continued, "I did pull off the threesome that I was telling you about with him and Trevor before dinner."

"I wanted to sneak away when we were in the restaurant to talk to you, but I didn't get the chance," Eden replied. "I'm dying to know… How was it?"

"It was absolutely amazing!" Julia giggled, "I'll tell you all about it. How about breakfast or lunch tomorrow?… Right now, my mind is totally on you."

She then flicked her tongue down the right side of Eden's neck, before gliding it across her plush red lips, and back into her mouth.

"God, I love the way you kiss," Eden whispered in a soft breathy voice.

Julia smiled to herself as she thought about Nurse Madison, and the way she has been coaching and helping her become a totally sexy dynamo. Of course, she also can't deny the role that Jordan has played in helping her embrace every ounce of her wild and sexy side as well.

"And I love everything about you, Officer Monroe," Julia replied, then added a little bite to Eden's bottom lip.

"Oh my God!… I love that!" Eden complimented her, "You are such a bad girl."

"I am a bad girl!" Julia replied with a sexy chuckle.

She quickly allowed her right hand to wander over the front of Eden's police uniform and gently began rubbing her vagina, as her left hand squeezed Eden's breast.

"Mmm," Eden immediately responded to Julia's sensual touches.

"Just so you know," Julia smirked at her, "Even though Jordan spanked me, I still want to be spanked by this sexy, totally-hot police officer whose lap I'm sitting on."

"You can count on that, babe," Eden smiled. "I can't wait to add my hand-prints all over those cute cheeks of yours! We promised them a show, and I can't wait until they see what I do to you."

She assertively grabbed Julia and pulled her closer. Both of Eden's pretty hands clenched tightly onto Julia's perfect little bubble of an ass, and once again, their tongues collided into another earth-shattering kiss.

Chapter 10

Their make-out session filled with passionate kisses went on for at least another twenty minutes until they both heard Rebecca emitting some very sexy moans from inside the bathroom.

"Looks like Jordan is really scrubbing her down," Eden cutely giggled as Rebecca's moans were now increasing in volume.

"Haha!" Julia laughed, "My guess is he's going down on her in the shower. He might even be fucking her in the ass. He loves that!"

"He's not the only one that loves that," Eden smirked, as her lips went right back to kissing Julia.

"Ahhh! Yes!... right there!... OOO! I'm coming!" Rebecca's voice carried all the way out into the hallway.

Julia was totally correct. As the warm water of the shower washed over Rebecca's long blond hair, Jordan was on his knees licking her pussy and bringing her to another amazing orgasm. Julia and Eden smiled at each other as they continued getting lost in their own soft passionate kisses. After a short while, Rebecca and Jordan came back into the living room wrapped with towels around their bodies.

Julia stopped her kiss and pulled away from Eden just long enough to ask.

"Have fun?"

Of course, Julia asked with that sly little devilish grin on her cute face.

"Oh my God!" Rebecca quickly answered, "His tongue should be illegal... And his dick is a masterpiece... I devoured him."

"Yummy!" Julia giggled, and then boldly asked Rebecca, "Did he fuck you in the ass?"

"God no! With the size of that cock?" Rebecca quickly chimed. "He fucked me so hard in the shower that it just about killed me!"

She then giggled and continued, "And even though I was gagging like crazy with his huge dick in my mouth, I managed to give him a blow job that he would always remember. Complete with my finger up his ass and swallowing every drop he gave me!"

"Good girl!" Julia quickly responded, "But whenever he does fuck you in the ass, I want to be there to watch!"

Rebecca nervously chuckled, "I've never done anal with a boy before, but if he promises to take it easy on me, I would love to try it with him someday soon."

"I promise that I'll go easy on you, Bec," Jordan quickly chimed in, "I can't wait to fuck that cute little ass of yours."

"Don't worry, I'll help coach you, Bec," Julia smiled at her cute friend. "But right now, I've got some unfinished business with this hot police officer."

"I suggest you guys take a seat," Eden called out to Rebecca and Jordan. "I'm about to take this naughty girl over my lap for a good hard spanking."

"I'm going to love seeing this!" Jordan commented.

He and Rebecca quickly took a seat on the sofa, as Eden sat herself down on the high-back wooden chair in the middle of the living room.

"Let's go, cutie," she tapped her hands on her lap, "Over my knee."

"Yes, Ma'am," Julia replied as she maneuvered herself into position on Eden's lap.

Her cute cheeks were already totally covered and marked with hand-prints by Jordan, but that didn't matter. Eden's sexy dark eyes gazed down at Julia's cute bare bottom perched across her knees like it was a piece of meat. She proactively took hold of Julia's right arm and pinned it behind her lower back, then clamped her right leg over both of Julia's legs. Eden then raised her hand high and delivered an intense flurry of slaps that made Julia instantly howl.

<SLAP><SLAP><SLAP>
<SLAP><SLAP>

"OW!.. OUCH!" Julia immediately yelped as her already tender cheeks felt the sting of Eden's unforgiving slaps.

<SLAP><SLAP><SLAP><SLAP>

"Ooo!… Yeow!" she squealed as Eden's strong hand continued to rain down with force on her backside.

With her mobility greatly limited, all Julia could do was cry out, clench her bare bottom, and slightly squirm over Eden's lap. Of course, looking down and seeing Julia squeeze her amazing little ass cheeks as tight as she could as a response to getting spanked only made Eden even more turned on. She tightened her legs and really clamped down with that scissors of a grip around Julia's cute thighs. Jordan and Rebecca couldn't help but enjoy the sight of seeing this absolutely stunning police woman giving Julia a serious bare bottom spanking.

Not only was Eden an incredibly strong and very capable spanker, she was also as hot as hell. She had his beyond stern expression and furrowed eyebrows painted on her pretty face that conveyed that she was in charge and meant business. Add to that, how she was fully dressed in her police uniform while Julia was completely naked, draped over her knee and you have the making of a scene so hot, that it would satisfy even the most picky and demanding spanking and fetish enthusiasts.

Jordan was really smiling from ear to ear as his dick, once again, was responding and growing underneath the towel wrapped around his body. Eden added one last dose of red hand-prints to Julia's tightly clenched ass, and even sent a few very hard slaps down the back of her thighs.

<SLAP><SLAP><SLAP>
<SLAP>

"Oooow!"

After that last flurry, Eden stopped and immediately stuck her index finger into her mouth to lubricate it with her own saliva. Without any further ado, she plunged her totally wet finger deep into Julia's rectum. Knowing how much Julia loved ass play, this sexy change-up made Julia instantly pant and take several deep breaths.

As Eden watched Julia wiggle and grind her sexy athletic body over her lap, she continued to finger fuck her rectum. Julia was now totally turned-on and called out in a very scratchy, labored voice.

"Oh my G-o-d!... That feels A-M-A-Z-I-N-G!"

Eden reveled in the way she was now making Julia moan with pleasure and how the young beauty was tightening her ass cheeks. Eden also loved the way Julia was gyrating her hips across her lap and grinding into her thighs. These sexy movements and hip gyrations that Julia was doing across Eden's lap gave a total picture of the way the young student could fuck like a rabbit.

Eden, looking down at this amazing sight, also loved feeling the wetness of Julia's vagina trickling onto her lap as well. She couldn't help but display a beautiful, yet condescending smile on her face as she continued to deeply finger Julia's cute asshole. She was careful not to overdo it, knowing that if she continued much longer, Julia would surely climax. She gave her one last hard finger fuck before she pulled Julia off her lap and onto her feet. The moment Eden got up to stand in front of her, Julia immediately started undressing her.

"I want to taste you so badly," Julia called out as her pretty hands began helping Eden remove her police uniform.

Eden also did her part and took off her own shoes and socks before stepping totally out of her uniform. In a matter of seconds, she completed the task by removing her panties and bra, which allowed her beautifully mature figure to be fully on display.

Julia's eyes feasted on Eden's completely toned and curvy physique, which was complimented by a number of amazingly sexy tattoos. Rebecca, who was watching together with Jordan, couldn't help but whisper to him about just how beautiful she thought Eden was. Jordan, of course, wholeheartedly agreed as his big green eyes took in every inch of Officer Eden Monroe's incredible body.

"You are breathtakingly beautiful," Jordan called out to her, as he watched Julia's talented tongue go straight to licking Eden's pussy.

Eden's hands took hold of the back of Julia's head as she now wiggled and gyrated her sexy body over Julia's tongue.

"Mmm!" Eden called out with pleasure.

"You taste amazing!" Julia quickly added as she continued to devour every drop of Eden's wetness.

Jordan and Rebecca were getting the show of their life as they continued to watch all the action unfold right before their eyes. Eden's sexy moans became elevated to another level when she felt Julia's finger plunge deep into her asshole. She tilted her head backwards, and allowed herself to get lost in the sensations that she was feeling from having Julia's magical tongue on her clit and her index finger penetrating her rectum.

"OOOooo!... Yes!" Eden squealed, "I love that! It feels insane!"

"Cum for me," Julia replied as she continued licking Eden's super-wet pussy.

"Not yet," Eden responded back in a totally out of breath voice. "There's more that I want to do with you!"

Eden then pointed to Jordan and commented in a very sexy voice, "And there is so much more that I want to do with you!"

She then smirked at Rebecca, "And you too!"

Chapter 11

Eden reached into her toy bag and pulled out even more kinky sex toys. She grabbed several vibrators along with dildos of various shapes, textures, and sizes, before leading Julia by the arm over to the sofa. She then signaled for Rebecca and Jordan to get up and switch places with them.

Rebecca and Jordan quickly moved to share a seat on an over-sized chair in the living room as Eden positioned Julia to lay flat on her back. Once she had Julia in the exact position that she wanted, she then maneuvered herself over her in the opposite direction to form the sixty-nine position. Eden's tongue immediately went to licking Julia's soaked pussy at the same time that Julia's tongue thoroughly licked every drop of Eden's wetness. Within seconds, both of them got totally lost in the taste of each other as they emitted some very sexy moans that totally filled the living room.

Eden kicked it up a notch when she turned on a small vibrator, and traced it across Julia's most sensitive areas. At the same time, she continued flicking her sexy tongue all over Julia's clitoris and made sure that she licked every single solitary drop of her young pussy. It took only a matter of seconds for Julia to call out.

"Oooh!... I'm close!"

"Not yet, babe," Eden quickly retracted and paused from all the action of pleasuring Julia.

"Take a deep breath and let it build," She coached Julia.

She then guided Julia onto her knees while positioning her torso over the back of the sofa. She positioned herself in the same exact way, kneeling, bent over the back of the sofa, and called out to Jordan and Rebecca in a very sexy and demanding voice.

"You two… bring your tongues over here!"

Eden's hands took hold of Julia's perfect ass and spread her cheeks as wide as she could, while she instructed Rebecca.

"Lick her like an ice cream cone."

Rebecca shed the towel that was wrapped around her body and took her position kneeling on the plush carpet. She immediately allowed her tongue to taste every drop of Julia's wetness. Once again, within seconds, Julia went right back to panting and breathing heavily.

"Oh my God, Bec!… Your tongue feels amazing," Julia blurted as she felt Rebecca flatten her tongue and lick all over her clitoris.

Eden added to the fire that Julia was feeling as she plunged her tongue deep into Julia's mouth. Julia was in heaven feeling the sensation of Rebecca performing oral on her, while at the same time having Eden kiss her with such passion. After a few more minutes, Eden signaled for Rebecca to stop as she called out to Jordan.

"Your turn, baby."

Jordan quickly removed the towel covering his lower body as his
talented tongue immediately picked up where Rebecca left off. He
totally devoured every drop of Julia's warm wetness. He also
added this cute little sucking sensation that he does over the lips
of her clitoris that really makes Julia totally flip out.

"OOOO!" Julia responded in a very labored voice.

Eden planted another sexy kiss on Julia's cute, soft red lips before
calling out to Rebecca again.

"Switch!"

Jordan gave way to let Rebecca once again take over the task of
giving Julia the oral satisfaction of her life. Julia's moans were
loud and clear as she quickly called out.

"I'm getting close... I can't hold it back!"

"Yes, you can, honey," Eden quickly replied and signaled for
Rebecca to stop.

"I'll give you a quick break," she commented to Julia, and then
called out to Rebecca and Jordan.

"My turn, for you two to work on me."

Eden signaled for Rebecca to go down on her as she pulled Jordan over and guided his tongue to lick her breasts and nipples. As Rebecca licked her pussy and Jordan licked her breasts, Eden turned on the small vibrator and held it firmly against her own vagina.

"OOoo!" she moaned as her beautiful body began to quiver.

"Switch!"

Once again, she called out making Jordan and Rebecca exchange positions.

Rebecca's tongue now glided over her nipples as Jordan got his first taste of Eden's thoroughly soaked pussy. He not only licked every centimeter of her clitoris, he also plunged his tongue deep into her pussy, and once again, he used that gentle suction that he'd perfected. Eden now moaned even louder as she experienced the talent of Jordan's oral skills.

It got even hotter as Jordan slid his tongue up the crack of her ass and rimmed her.

"OOOOO!" Eden wiggled and squirmed as her moans filled the room.

"Okay, Stop!"

She quickly called out as she came close to climaxing. Eden took a moment and paused, allowing herself to recover for a bit. She did this to build an even stronger climax, knowing this temporary delay would be well worth it when the time came for her to explode into an epic orgasm. She called out to Julia as she came off the sofa, grabbed a large double-sided dildo, and positioned herself on the carpet of the living room.

"Now, we are really going to fuck each other!" She smirked as she took hold of Julia's hand.

Eden guided Julia's athletic legs to open wide as she inserted the end of the dildo deep inside of her. She then did the same to herself and guided the opposite end of the pretty pink, jelly-like dildo, inside her own pussy.

Jordan and Rebecca, once again, got to watch an incredibly sexy show as they took in the sight of Eden totally gyrating and thrusting her hips, while at the same time, coaching Julia to do the same. Eden pulled Julia even closer to her as she kissed her with a raging fire, then whispered.

"Grind it… Hard and fast!"

She demonstrated, as she feverishly took hold of part of the dildo that was sticking out of her vagina and used her hand to stroke and add to the thrusting. Julia took the cue, followed her lead, and did the same thing as her head quickly tilted back from the amazing sensation.

"OOoo!… Yes!" Julia called out.

"Now you can orgasm!" Eden coached her. "Grind it… Hard!"

Eden was now fiercely grinding and thrusting the dildo in a way that not only made it feel amazing to herself, but also made Julia's vagina tingle with delight. Julia experienced total euphoria as she tightened her Kegel muscles and felt every fiber in her young body explode into an earth-shattering orgasm.

"Oh my God!... Yes!... I'm coming!" Julia called out as her tight little body shook rapidly.

Eden stopped gyrating, but gave one hard thrust that made the dildo penetrate as deep as possible into Julia's vagina, making sure she climaxed into an orgasm that she would never forget. Julia moaned loudly as she trembled and erupted like a volcano.

Once she came back down to earth, she quickly responded.

"Phew!... Holy fuck, that was intense!... You are amazing!"

Eden smiled at Julia's compliment and slid her tongue slowly across Julia's lips, giving her another very sexy kiss.

"And you, my dear, are one sexy little girl!" Eden replied with a cute smirk.

She proceeded and removed the dildo, which made Julia instantly respond.

"Hey! No fair... You didn't orgasm!" Julia looked at Eden with confusion. "I want to get you off!"

"Oh, don't worry, baby. You're going to help me have an amazing orgasm," Eden quickly replied with a smile. "Actually, you all are… I'm just letting it build!"

Chapter 12

Jordan took it upon himself and now stepped forward. He planted a very steamy kiss on Eden's lips as his hands grabbed and squeezed her perfectly plump ass.

"I'll get you off!" he boldly whispered to her, as his super-erect cock pressed against her left leg.

"So… You have an agreement with your husband not to have sex with me…" he continued to tease Eden, "Does anal count?… Because I would love nothing more than to fuck this beautiful ass of yours!"

"Sorry, handsome," Eden smiled at him, "I would love to have your dick in my ass and to also have you fuck me every way possible, but I have to honor the agreement that I made with my husband."

"Eden, we'll never tell," Julia quickly chimed.

Eden smiled and clearly explained, "Having complete trust in each other is the only way an open marriage can work… At least for Zach and I. We are not all-out swingers. This is something we do selectively… for fun. It's something we do to enhance our marriage and I'm not going to risk it."

"I respect you, and your decision," Jordan replied displaying a slight frown on his face. "But in the future, if Zach ever allows it, I am going to fuck you senseless!… He can even watch!"

Eden laughed out loud and replied, "Hell no!… If I get that chance, I want you alone… One on one!"

Julia quickly chimed in, "Well if you offer your husband a night with Rebecca and I, hopefully he'll give you the go ahead with Jordan."

"Oh, he definitely will!" Eden smiled and gave Jordan a sexy look, "I promise you, handsome... The next time we get together, I'll be riding that dick of yours!"

"Deal!" Jordan immediately embraced her with another super-passionate kiss, then quickly dropped to his knees and slid his tongue all over the inside of her thighs. He continued to really tease Eden and gloss over her most sensitive areas by giving several stray licks to her clitoris.

"Oh my God!… You're tongue feels A-M-A-Z-I-N-G!" Eden called out in the sexiest of moans.

Julia quickly followed his lead and slid her tongue down Eden's neck and over her breast. She then signaled for Rebecca to come over and kiss Eden as well.

"All three of us will work on every inch of your body and do whatever you want," Julia whispered as Rebecca's tongue now licked the opposite side of Eden's neckline.

"Damn right you will!" Eden smirked and replied, "But first, I have a few more tricks up my sleeve."

Eden smiled as she took hold of Rebecca's wrist, while she gave Jordan a very sexy look, and announced, "I'm not done with the two of you."

"Follow me!" she called out as she grabbed her toy bag, and started walking Rebecca in the direction of the bedroom.

Once inside the bedroom, Eden led Rebecca over to the bed and guided her to lay horizontally across it. She immediately took her position kneeling on the carpet as her hands guided Rebecca's legs to open wide. Eden's tongue went straight for Rebecca's clitoris and within a few seconds, Rebecca was completely moist all over again.

"Mmm… Oh my God!" her young, withered voice called out as she felt the magic of Eden's tongue.

"Rollover… Onto your tummy," Eden instructed her.

Rebecca quickly followed Eden's instructions and the minute she turned onto her stomach, Eden's hands grabbed hold of her legs and guided them into the spread eagle position. Without wasting a second, Eden slid her tongue right into the crack of Rebecca's cute ass and started to rimming her asshole.

"Ooooh!" Rebecca immediately responded.

Julia and Jordan stood right next to them, taking in all the action of Eden totally devouring Rebecca's tight body.

"Get on all fours," Eden called out to Rebecca as she helped guide her into the exact position that she wanted her in.

She then reached into her toy bag and retrieved a tube of KY jelly, along with several different sized butt plugs. Eden thoroughly lubricated the smaller butt plug and handed it to Jordan.

"Hold this," she instructed him as she proceeded to lubricate the other slightly larger one.

After that anal plug was sufficiently lubricated, she passed it to Julia and announced, "You hold this one."

Eden then applied a generous amount of lubricant all over her index finger, and even dabbed some directly on Rebecca's anal opening.

"I want you to relax and take a deep breath," she coached Rebecca, as her index finger now teased the opening of Rebecca's anus.

Rebecca followed through and the moment she took a nice deep breath, Eden gently inserted her finger into her rectum.

"OOoo!" Rebecca gasped and took another deep breath.

"Good girl," Eden coached, "Keep taking some nice steady deep breaths and don't clench your butt."

Rebecca listened and got into a rhythm with her breathing as she felt Eden's finger now deeply penetrating her rectum.

"Oooh! That feels so good!" Rebecca responded through her heavy breathing.

"I'm going nice and easy, then I'm going to use a small butt plug on you," Eden explained.

After several addition minutes of probing Rebecca's rectum, Eden removed her finger. She cleansed it with an alcohol pad, before taking the small butt plug from Jordan. Rebecca remained in position, kneeling on all fours on top of the bed. He kept her head down low, and her cute little ass high in the air.

"Deep breath, Becca," Eden announced as she gently inserted the small butt plug.

"Ouch!" Rebecca first called out, then relaxed as the anal plug penetrated her rectum.

"There… That's it… Good girl," Eden continued to coach her as she now walked around the other side of the bed to give Rebecca a steamy kiss.

"Mmm!" Rebecca quickly responded as she experienced the taste of Eden's tongue in addition to the anal plug in her rectum.

After their sexy kiss, Eden signaled Jordan over as she walked away.

"Kiss her with everything you got," she instructed Jordan.

Jordan allowed his hands to gently massage Rebecca's perky breast as he engulfed her in a kiss that was so hot it had Rebecca quivering in place. At the same time, Eden was now moving the butt plug slowly, in and out, of Rebecca's anus, while her left hand gently rubbed Rebecca's super-moist pussy.

"Whooa!" Rebecca called out as the mixture of sensations totally blew her mind.

"Keep breathing, Rebecca," Eden coached her, "Nice and steady."

"God, this feels amazing!" Rebecca responded as she took in the taste of Jordan's tongue in addition to the anal plug and the soft touches from both of their hands.

Eden now signaled for Julia to come over with the slightly larger anal plug. As she removed the small butt plug, she gave a nod of her head for Julia to insert that butt plug into Rebecca's rectum.

"Nice and slow," Eden instructed Julia, as she once again called out to Rebecca. "Take a nice deep breath."

Again, Rebecca followed Eden's guidance as she felt Julia insert the slightly larger butt plug into her rectum. Jordan added to her pleasure and gave her another kiss which made her moan even louder.

"Mmmm!"

"Keep moving it in and out slowly," Eden instructed Julia, as she reached into her toy bag.

Both Jordan and Julia's eyes lit up like fireworks as they watched Eden slip on a strap-on and fasten it around her hips. Rebecca, who was still facing forward, had no idea what Eden was planning next. Without saying a word, Eden gave a hand signal for Julia to remove the anal plug as she thoroughly lubricated a small dildo and snapped it in place onto the strap-on harness. She took a moment to whisper some instructions into Julia's ear, which in turn made Julia smile from ear to ear, as she went off and quickly dove her hands into Eden's sexy bag of tricks.

Chapter 13

Eden flashed Julia that devilish smile of hers as she watched her follow instructions and retrieve the additional items she whispered to her from the bag. She proceeded to stay hidden from Rebecca's view as she approached her from behind. Jordan was also doing his part as he kept Rebecca distracted by planting another steamy kiss, while moving his hands downward to rub her clitoris, and finger her pussy.

Rebecca was now really breathing heavily as Jordan continued to kiss and finger her pussy. The very next thing she felt was Eden's hands on her ass cheeks, spreading them far apart. While Eden's hands held Rebecca's ass open as wide as she could, she gently inserted the tip of the dildo into her anus. Eden then took hold of Rebecca's outer thighs, coaching her once again as she slowly began gyrating her hips.

"Take a very deep breath, Rebecca."

"Oow!"

Once again, Rebecca expressed a slight discomfort as the dildo penetrated her rectum.

"Relax, babe... I promise it's going to feel amazing," Eden assured her.

Eden continued to gently thrust her hips to make sure the lubrication was making its way all through Rebecca's rectum. She quickly received confirmation as Rebecca now started to emit some very sexy moans.

"Mmmm!" Rebecca sounded off with delight.

Once Eden felt Rebecca totally relax, she slowly began to increase the force of her thrusts. She moved her hands upwards to tightly hold onto the sides of Rebecca's hips and started pounding her with more force each time. It didn't take long for Rebecca to totally moan with pleasure.

"Oooh!... God Y-E-S!"

Her young body was overwhelmed as she experienced this level of anal penetration for the first time. Eden actually signaled for Jordan to stop fingering her pussy so that Rebecca could focus on the pleasure her ass was feeling.

Eden continued to hold onto Rebecca's young hips with the force of a vice-grip as she now really pounded her. Every thrust of Eden's mature, curvy hips was hard, deep and very deliberate. Since she was using the smallest size anal dildo, these thrusts made way more sound than they did impact. However, for a first timer like Rebecca, this was the perfect introduction to anal sex.

"OOoo!" Rebecca's sexy moans along with the sound of their bodies slapping against each other echoed loudly off the walls of the bedroom.

After a few more sexy thrusts using all the force she could, Eden slowly pulled out and stepped away. She then gave Julia the signal, who was standing by with a strap-on harness as well. The harness Julia was wearing had a slightly larger dildo mounted on it. Eden quickly assisted as she gripped Rebecca's ass cheeks and spread them open as wide as possible for Julia.

Julia nodded and gave her a cute little smirk, before proceeding and gently invading Rebecca's anus with the strap-on dildo.

"Ouch!… Ooo!"

Once again, Rebecca first felt a slight pain from the dildo penetrating her asshole. After about a minute or so of allowing the lubrication to fully work with her body, Rebecca then made it perfectly clear that she was feeling complete euphoria. Julia loved hearing her cute friend moan with pleasure like this, especially since she was the reason Rebecca was losing all control. Julia then kicked it up a notch and really fucked Rebecca's ass even harder.

"Mmmm!… Oooh!"

"Breath, Bec," Julia instructed her, as she delivered some seriously forceful thrusts.

Jordan couldn't help but smile from ear to ear watching Rebecca moan loudly as she got her ass fucked by Julia while Eden continued to hold her cheeks open. It sure was one hell of a sight to take in.

"Good job!" Eden replied with a smirk towards Julia. "Fuck this cute ass of hers with everything you got!"

After another minute or two of getting her ass totally reamed, Rebecca screamed out, "Mmmm!… I'm close."

Eden quickly stepped away to retrieve her favorite vibrator. It was a large wand type unit with a round head that resembled a tennis ball. She quickly turned it on to a medium setting and held it firmly against Rebecca's clitoris. She then instructed Julia one last time.

"Harder!"

Julia nodded and literally slammed her body with full force against Rebecca's. She really fucked her ass hard and with the speed of a wild jack rabbit. Rebecca was now soaking wet with sweat as she felt the tender sensations of Eden holding the vibrator to her clit, mixed with the intensity of Julia fucking her ass.

"Ooh!… Yes!" She yelled out as Eden moved the vibrator in small circles.

"God Y-E-S…. I'm coming!"

Rebecca's announcement made Julia deliver one last forceful thrust of maximum impact with the strap-on as she gripped Rebecca's hips and held it deep inside of her.

"Ahhhh!" Rebecca screamed as her tight athletic body climaxed, then shook rapidly.

The cute young student continued to emit some very sexy moans as she exploded into an orgasm unlike any that she had ever experienced.

Eden made sure to hold the vibrator in place until every bit of Rebecca's orgasm ended, and her body totally stopped quivering. When that finally happened, Eden pulled the vibrator away, turned it off, then gave the signal for Julia to slowly pull out of Rebecca.

The very moment that Julia did that, Rebecca totally collapsed flat in the prone position on top of the bed.

"Oh my God!… I'm spent!" she quickly announced, then flipped over to look up at Eden and Julia.

"That was the best E-V-E-R!" Rebecca gleamed with excitement as she now smiled at them.

Eden gave her a cute little comforting kiss and sardonically replied, "Congrats, babe! You can now say that you've been fucked in the ass."

Eden's sarcastic humor made everyone in the bedroom laugh out loud. She then turned to Jordan with a slight perplexed look on her face.

"Well champ, my intentions were to also have you fuck Rebecca's ass, but as you witnessed, she couldn't hold on long enough. And it's safe to say that she's probably going to be a little sore back there for a day or two."

Jordan laughed and replied, "That's cool. I enjoyed every bit of watching it all go down."

"Next time, my ass is yours, Jordan," Rebecca chuckled and followed up with. "Only if you promise to start slowly like they did."

"Of course," Jordan smirked back at her.

"You're not leaving me out of this," Julia quickly chimed, "I loved doing this so much, that I'm going to buy this exact strap-on."

"It's yours babe," Eden replied, "Keep it. I don't use that one much, since I have a couple more in my bag that can adjust to various sizes. Just remember to always sterilize it thoroughly, and you can even put a condom over it like I did."

"I need another shower," Rebecca laughed. "You guys gave me quite a workout. I'm still sweating like crazy!"

As Rebecca exited the bedroom on route to the bathroom, Eden proceeded to clean her strap on. She then handed Julia a disinfectant wipe as well, before giving her a well-deserved compliment.

"You were amazing, Julia," Eden smiled at her. "Was that the first time you ever used a strap-on?"

"Yeah," Julia giggled, "It was… But I've watched a lot of porn, and I was dying to do this… I especially want to do this to him."

Julia pointed to Jordan with that devilish smile on her face.

"I was going to buy a strap-on like this and plot my revenge on him sometime this week. I planned on tying him up and fucking his ass hard, the way he always fucks mine!"

Julia's admission immediately made Jordan smile as he playfully stuck his tongue out at her.

Eden reached into her bag of tricks, and once again, retrieved her handcuffs. She walked over to Jordan and snapped one of the handcuffs onto his right wrist as she pulled him toward the edge of the bed.

"No time like the present," she announced.

"Ready to get your ass fucked, Jordan?" Eden smirked at him.

"Doesn't seem like I have much of a choice," he responded.

"You don't!" Eden bantered back at him, as she weaved the other handcuff through the railing of the bed before locking it over his left wrist.

Chapter 14

Eden unsnapped the small dildo from her harness only to replace it with dildo attachment that was slightly larger. She proceeded to thoroughly lubricate this dildo with the KY jelly before handing the tube to Julia. Julia quickly did the same and generously lubricated the dildo that she was wearing as well. She then nodded her head and handed the tube back to Eden.

Eden now approached Jordan with the tube of KY jelly in her hand. She had that sexy, cunning look all across her face that didn't even come close to concealing her excitement. She stared down at his totally bruised ass as he was handcuffed and bent over the back of the bed.

"Mmm… Mmm… Mmm," she mumbled in an insanely sexy tone. "Such an amazing ass!"

Her right hand now playfully added a few squeezes along with several pats to Jordan's completely marked rear-end.

"We have so much in common, Jordan," Eden teased him, as she gave his bare bottom a good hard pinch

"Not only do I love spanking… I equally love fucking beautiful asses!"

Julia quickly added, "His ass is about as beautiful as there is for a guy."

"It sure is," Eden smirked back as she squeezed and fondled his bare bottom again.

She then stepped in front of him and lifted his chin with her finger.

"I'm going to L-O-V-E fucking your ass!" Eden smirked, as she proceeded to apply the KY jelly generously to her right index finger.

She made sure to do this right in front of Jordan's face to make sure his eyes took in the sight of her lubricating her pretty finger.

"No one has ever done this to me," Jordan admitted, feeling a bit scared and tense.

"Don't worry baby, we'll take it easy on you," Eden replied. "At least at first!"

"Uuh!" Jordan gasped as Eden forcefully plunged her index finger straight into his asshole.

Her pretty finger penetrated him hard and deep, making him gasp for breath.

"That a boy," she teased him as her entire mouth engulfed his left ear. She followed it up with a sarcastic whisper.

"You better breathe deep and relax. Is that clear?"

"Yes, Ma'am!" Jordan answered in a completely shaky voice.

Eden was now really violating his asshole, as she continued to finger him hard and deep.

"Oooh!" Jordan moaned loudly.

Moaning was about all he could do, since he remained handcuffed and bent-over the bed. Just then Rebecca came back into the bedroom fresh from her shower and just in time to catch all the action. Feeling more than spent and completely satisfied, she stood silently against the wall enjoying the view.

Eden glanced over at Rebecca and smiled as she gave Jordan's cute, tight ass one last forceful finger-fuck. She then removed her finger and signaled for Julia. Julia wasted no time as she grabbed Jordan's hips and mounted him. She guided the tip of the dildo to his asshole, and then gyrated her hips with a hard thrust, making it penetrate his anus.

"Ooow!" Jordan called out, as he felt the force of the dildo enter his rectum.

"Breathe baby," Eden quickly coached him.

She then gave Julia an approving nod, and before you know it, Julia was working the strap-on like a champ and pounding the daylights out of the guy she was so in love with.

"Uuuh… Mmm!" Jordan now let out a few sexy moans that

immediately made Julia want to hear more.

"Moan for me, baby," Julia called out to him, "Let me hear you!"

She really kicked it up a notch as her tight little body slammed with force against his ass cheeks.

"I'm going to fuck your ass the way you fuck mine!" Julia replied as she added a few hard hand slaps across his right butt cheek.

"OOoo!" Jordan's moans bounced off the walls of the bedroom.

He wasn't the only one turned on, as Julia's pussy was now throbbing and dripping wet from using the strap-on to fuck his tight muscular ass.

"Mmmm!" her moans now echoed in unison with his.

Eden didn't want Julia to climax, as she still had other plans for her. She tapped Julia on the shoulder and wisely called out.

"My turn to get at his ass!"

Julia gave a few more extremely hard thrusts that had Jordan gasping for air before she pulled the strap-on out of him. Eden quickly smiled at Julia as she announced.

"You can take that off... I have plans for you!"

Julia followed her instruction and removed the harness, then took her position, standing next to Rebecca. Without wasting another second, Eden removed the handcuffs and escorted Jordan to lie flat on his back on top of the bed.

She handed Julia her wand vibrator and instructed her to hold it until she called for it. She then lifted Jordan's muscular legs upward to just about resemble the diaper position as she held them in place.

"Take a deep breath, baby," she told him as her hands lined up the tip of the dildo to his asshole.

The moment Jordan took a deep breath, Eden gave a little thrust, and just like that, the slightly larger dildo penetrated his asshole. She started slowly gyrating her hips to make it go deeper and deeper with each thrust.

Jordan was now letting out some of the sexiest moans he ever made as the older, super-sophisticated bombshell gave his ass the fucking of his life. After starting out gently, Eden was now pounding him with just about everything she had.

Rebecca and Julia got to witness the sex show of their life as Eden totally dominated Jordan's mind, body, and soul.

"MMM!… Oooh!" he moaned with pleasure. "That feels so fucking G-O-O-D!"

"Cum for me!" Eden replied to him as she really fucked his ass hard.

She then signaled for Julia to come over with the wand. She directed her to turn the vibrator on low, and hold it firmly against Jordan's super-tight testicles. Eden then used her right hand to grab the shaft of his massive cock and started to vigorously stroke it as she continued to fuck him with the strap-on.

This double-team effort took all of about 30 seconds before Jordan caved in, called out, and totally exploded.

"Ahhhh!… Yes!… I'm coming!"

Eden gave one last forceful thrust and pressed her body as hard as she could into him. The dildo was buried deep into his rectum as her skillful hand stroked him to ecstasy. Julia did her part and kept the vibrator firmly pressed onto his testicles.

"Oooo!… FUCK YES!" he moaned.

Jordan experienced total euphoria as his sperm shot out with the force of a cannonball all over his six-pack abs. Eden continued, and didn't stop milking him until she was sure every last drop of semen had exited his body.

Once Jordan's body stopped shaking, she gave Julia the nod to turn the vibrator off and pull it away. She then took a moment and slowly removed the dildo from his rectum. The minute she did, she tossed the condom covering the dildo in the garbage, before leaning down to give Jordan a sexy, well-deserved kiss.

"That was fucking intense!" Jordan quickly complimented them. "You both are amazing!"

"You're A-M-A-Z-I-N-G!" Eden complimented him back. "I can't wait to have you fuck me!"

Of course, Jordan couldn't help delivering one of his cocky responses.

"I am going to F-U-C-K every single hole in your body!" he smirked, "You're going to forget all about your husband!"

"I'm counting on that baby..." Eden replied. "But right now, It's my turn to orgasm and all of you are going to help."

Chapter 15

Eden didn't let another moment pass as she grabbed Julia and escorted her onto the bed. She maneuvered her into the same exact position that Jordan was just in, lying flat on her back with her legs up in the air. Julia's pretty face looked up at Eden and watched intently as she snapped a larger dildo onto her harness.

Eden then called out instructions. She first looked over at Rebecca, and literally threw a latex glove at her. She then instructed her.

"Becca, when I give you the word, I want you to finger my ass... hard and deep!"

Eden then glanced over at Jordan and instructed him.

"And I want you to lick my pussy with that amazing tongue of yours!"

Eden now focused her attention on Julia as she looked down at her on top of the bed. She displayed that pretty but devious trademark of a smile across her face. Her right hand quickly began petting Julia's already moist vagina as she told her.

"As for you, you sexy little feisty girl... I'm going to fuck you silly!"

"Oh my God!" Julia moaned back at her. "I'm so fucking wet that I'm about to cum any second!"

With that announcement, Eden tightly gripped Julia's muscular thighs, and with a hard thrusting motion, she plunged the dildo into her wet pussy.

"Oooh!… God, Y-E-S!" Julia immediately responded as Eden began fucking her with the strap-on.

In a matter of seconds, Eden fucked Julia so hard that Julia was totally gasping for air. Eden knew Julia was close, as she herself was approaching a much-needed orgasm. She penetrated Julia's young pussy as deep as possible and then kept the dildo thoroughly buried in her as she turned the vibrator on. Eden continued to hold it firmly against Julia's clitoris until she moaned.

"Oh My G-O-D!… Yes!. I'm coming!" Julia immediately announced as her entire body quivered into an amazing orgasm.

Eden now called out to Rebecca and Jordan to cater to her, as she continued to hold the vibrator in place until Julia reached her full climax.

She timed it about as perfect as can be. Julia's body slowly came off of cloud nine, which allowed Eden to concentrate on her own needs. With the dildo still buried inside Julia, Eden spread her legs as Jordan took a kneeling position. He immediately went to work with his talented tongue and started licking Eden's delicious pussy in every direction. Rebecca added to the sensation and plunged her gloved index finger deep into Eden's ass.

"Ahhh! Y-E-S!" Eden screamed. "MMMM!"

Julia managed to sit-up slightly, and just enough to reach Eden and plant a sexy kiss on her plush lips. She held her tight as Eden now trembled to her climax.

"OOOOh!" Eden moaned as Jordan sucked every drop of wetness out of her pussy.

Once her orgasm ended, Eden gave a nod for them to stop as she step back and removed the dildo out of Julia's vagina.

"That was the best E-V-E-R!" Eden announced. "And trust me... I've had my share of orgasms!"

After she embraced and thanked everyone, Eden called out with a giggle.

"My turn to take a shower and sterilize everything."

Rebecca gave her one last kiss, along with everyone else, before she got dressed and exited Julia's apartment. After several minutes, Eden emerged squeaky clean and proceeded to get dressed and gather her belongings.

"I can't thank you enough," Julia smiled and hugged her. "This was the best night ever!"

"It was your plan, babe," Eden complimented her. "You are one of the sexiest girls I've ever met… Embrace it!"

Eden followed it up with a compliment to Jordan as well, "And as for you… You are way too sexy for your own good… I can't wait to feel you inside me!"

Jordan smiled as he gave her a warm hug. Then, together with Julia, they walked Eden to the door. Once Eden exited the apartment, Julia threw herself into Jordan's muscular arms.

"That was beyond insane!… Did you enjoy it?" she looked up at him with her arms draped over his broad shoulders.

"Are you kidding?" Jordan smiled. "I fucking loved it… All of it!… Especially the way you pounded my ass with that strap-on!"

"There's more where that came from, baby. I loved doing it to you," Julia chimed.

"Let's take a shower, get some ice cream, then go to bed… I'm totally S-P-E-N-T!" she emphasized.

"Deal!" Jordan responded. "Just so you know… You amaze me! The way you planned all this and how absolutely sexy you are… Totally blows me away!"

Julia smiled back at him, and of course, had kept it a secret that Nurse Madison has been instrumental in helping her discover many parts of her sexuality, as well as to better understand her own body. Little does she know that Jordan already knew all about this, and that he and Nurse Madison have been hot and heavy, having a secret affair of their own.

She kissed him again, and added, "This surprise was the least I could do since you gave me the threesome that I was craving with you and Trevor."

"That was quite a shocker, babe," Jordan half-smiled.

"You handled it well… I was afraid you would totally freak out," Julia chuckled back at him. "So, I wanted to return the favor and give you an experience that you would always remember."

"That you did, baby," he smiled. "That you did!"

Chapter 16

"I'll get the shower started," Julia replied.

"Hold on," Jordan announced. "I have one more birthday present for you."

Jordan reached into his gym bag and pulled out a beautifully wrapped small box.

"Really?" Julia, totally surprised, responded. "You already gave me enough with the necklace and dinner, babe."

Jordan gave her a nod as she proceeded to open the present. Inside she found her favorite perfume combined with a matching bath set. It was complete with bubble bath, body butter, and facial moisturizer.

"Oh my God!" Julia screamed. "This is my favorite!"

"You always smell amazing, and your skin always feels so soft," Jordan smiled. "Rebecca, told me this was your favorite."

"Awww... Thank you, baby."

"You're welcome, Sweetheart," Jordan replied. "I say we take a bubble bath instead of a shower. I just need to check my messages and make sure work didn't call me."

"A warm bubble-bath sounds great!" Julia smiled. "I love that idea. I'll get it started. Don't make me wait too long."

As Julia went off to get the bath started, Jordan grabbed his cell phone and secretly sent a quick text message to Nurse Madison that read:

"Your private lessons have really made a huge difference with Julia. That was one hell of a surprise!"

Nurse Madison immediately texted back:

"Call me in the morning and come over for breakfast. I can't wait to hear all about it."

Jordan responded back with a thumbs up emoji, then shut his cell phone off and headed into the bathroom.

After a night of a well-deserved sleep and waking up in each other's arms, Julia grabbed a quick morning shower. She then headed out to meet her mom for the day. Jordan got in a quick morning workout, before returning to his dorm apartment. After a shower of his own, he changed into his favorite pair of ripped jeans and texted Nurse Madison that he was on his way to her house.

After about a twenty-minute drive, Jordan did the usual routine. He inconspicuously pulled his car into her garage before quickly hitting the remote to close the garage door. He politely removed his shoes as he entered into the kitchen of her upscale-condo.

"Hi, handsome!" Nurse Madison, who was making coffee, immediately greeted him with a smile followed by a sexy kiss.

Unlike Jordan, who was fully dressed, Madison was wearing a thick flannel shirt that just about covered herself. She looked beyond sexy as Jordan's hands immediately slid underneath the shirt to grab hold of her plump ass.

"You are so fucking hot," he commented as he now slid his hands underneath her panties to really squeeze her ass.

"So, I just got off the phone with Julia," Nurse Madison admitted. "She told me every detail. It sounds like you had the time of your life last night."

"It was absolutely insane!" Jordan replied. "I almost bailed on the Trevor threesome, but then I got into watching Julia with him… Crazy, right?"

"No, honey. It's not crazy at all. Many of us like watching," she smirked at him. "I would have loved to witness it. Especially watching them spank you and then fuck you in the ass. That alone would have made me climax."

Jordan giggled at Madison's admission.

"So tell about Eden… Julia flipped over her. She said she was as hot as fire."

"That she was," Jordan replied. "And she's a cop!… Fucking

insane!"

"I can't believe Julia found her on the website," Madison commented.

"Yeah, turns out she has a profile with her husband," Jordan replied. "They have an open marriage with respectable limits. Julia met them a few times for coffee and planned everything."

"Damn!... I need to get on that website," Madison joked, as she dropped to her knees and unfastened the button on the waistband of Jordan's faded jeans.

"Breakfast is going to have to wait," she smiled as she looked up at him.

Her pretty hands took hold of his jeans together with his underwear and gave an assertive tug that made them fall to his ankles. She then cupped his testicles and gave them a sexy squeeze as her entire mouth took in the shaft of his penis.

It took all of 5 seconds of feeling her tongue on his dick for Jordan's to grow into a full-on erection.

"Mmm... Now that's more like it," Madison smiled as she now started stroking him and tracing her tongue up and down the shaft of his cock.

"I want to see what she did to your ass," Madison commented, and spun him around to take in the full sight of his thoroughly bruised rear-end.

"Oh my!… Eden definitely has some spanking skills," Madison chuckled as her hands squeezed Jordan's tender cheeks.

"She's no stranger to giving spankings," Jordan smirked. "I can't wait to get revenge on her ass."

Madison quickly spun him back around and literally devoured his entire cock in her mouth. Jordan's head immediately tilted backward as he let out an incredibly sexy moan. As erect as his dick was, Madison did her best to take in just about the entire shaft of his penis before she pulled it out and licked it like a Lollipop.

"Mmm! That feels amazing!" Jordan commented as once again her mouth sucked on his massive cock.

"I'm close."

Jordan's entire body tensed up as he continued to moan and approached ejaculation.

"Give it all to me," Madison commented as her hands tightly held onto his ass cheeks while her fingernails dug in to pinch him.

"Ahhhh! Mmm!"

Just as Jordan called out, Madison plunged her index finger forcefully into his asshole. She continued to hold him in place as

Jordan exploded like a volcano into her mouth.

"Oooh! Y-E-S!" he moaned loudly as his body shook like a bowl of Jello.

Nurse Madison's right finger continued to be buried deep in his rectum as her left hand was tightly gripping and pinching his tender ass.

"Oow!" Jordan let out one final moan as she sucked every last drop of sperm out of him before she swallowed.

"Mmm!" she looked up with a smile. "You taste phenomenal!"

Jordan couldn't help but smile as he hoisted her up and literally placed her on top of the kitchen counter. He aggressively yanked her panties off her toned legs and buried his face deep into her pussy. His tongue went straight to doing its magic, flicking, sucking, and licking her clitoris over and over.

It took all of about two minutes before Madison moaned, "God Y-E-S... Right there... I'm coming!"

Just as she did to him, Jordan held onto her with a super-firm grip until he sucked every drop of her moisture out of her. Once her orgasm was over and her body stopped shaking, she hugged him tightly and joked.

"So, pancakes, French toast, an omelet?"

"You should know better than to ask me something like that," Jordan bantered back at her. "All of them!"

"Hahaha," Madison laughed and added. "In that case, we'll make it really sinful with chocolate chips and whipped cream."

Chapter 17

The old saying "Time waits for no one" was completely accurate and just like that, a couple of weeks had passed. Things were great and went right back to normal for Jordan, Julia, and even Rebecca. It was now mid-semester with holidays and a school break approaching. It's the time of year that many teachers schedule important exams and surprise pop-up tests that really makes the students anxiety levels fly off the charts. Even though they look forward to getting a few days off from school during this break, the students hate the stress of preparing for these tests.

Jordan and Julia continue to immerse themselves in their studies at The Academy, as well as work at their part-time jobs on campus. Their relationship still remains non-exclusive, and so far no one has a clue about Jordan and Nurse Madison's secret affair. Julia has also secretly continued her one-on-one mentoring with Nurse Madison, along with continuing her friends-with-benefits relationship with Rebecca. She's also been flirting with Trevor quite a bit, but has yet to hook-up with him again.

The reason for that was Julia used any additional free time that she had to keep in touch and meet-up with Eden. The two of them met for lunch a few times and have been busy orchestrating plans for their next sexy, all-in, get together. This hot scenario would include her and Rebecca having a threesome with Eden's husband Zach, while Eden has permission for an uninhibited, no-restrictions night with Jordan. Needless to say, Eden was salivating at the very thought of this, even more so than her husband, who would basically be getting a two-for-one deal.

The only complication was to work out the actual scheduling of this epic event. A number of things such as the school workload for the three students, along with the busy demands of Eden being a police officer, and the demands of her husband's corporate job, took first priority. Even with that, Eden and Julia did come up with a few possible days and times that could work for all of them in about a month or so, possibly over the Christmas break. In the meantime, she and Julia managed to have a couple of one-on-one hook-ups that were as hot as a raging inferno.

To say that they really enjoy turning each other on would be a total understatement. They actually excel at fulfilling each other's needs. Eden hadn't hesitated one bit in giving young Julia the discipline spankings that she craved so much from a stern, older woman. She has hand-spanked, paddled and strapped Julia's cute ass in just about every position imaginable. These hook-ups always make Julia feel the gambit of emotions as she first cries her eyes out from Eden's harsh spankings, before she experiences the total pleasure of an orgasm from her sensual skills.

On the flip side, Julia has given Eden the exact oral and penetration satisfaction that she loves so much. Julia's skills at oral sex and rimming, in addition to the way her young athletic body has been fucking Eden senseless with a variety of strap-on dildos, has really sent Eden into orbit.

She also loves sitting on Julia's face, smothering her with her plump ass, as she feels Julia's talented tongue probing her most intimate areas. Eden always pushes it right to the edge of a climax before she stops Julia and gets into position on all fours. From there, she yelps like an excited kid on Christmas morning as Julia mounts her from behind. Julia then proceeds to fuck her so hard, and so fast, that every rabbit on the planet would be envious. It usually takes Julia three to four minutes of non-stop, all-out cardio thrusting, before she makes Eden gush like a waterfall into a larger-than-life orgasm.

The two of them have also used just about every vibrator, harness, sex toy, and implement on each other that they can think of. In addition to all of this, Eden has even captured some of their escapades on video. Of course, she and Julia have vowed to keep this a total secret and have only used the video to enhance the times when they can't hook-up and have to resort to playing with themselves.

Just then, Julia's phone rings. She glances at it and sees that it's Eden calling.

"Hey!" she answers with a whisper of excitement.

"Hey yourself, cutie. How are you?" Eden replies. "Any chance you're free tonight? I'm off and Zach just got called into the office to work on a computer issue."

"Shit! I would love to, but I'm actually in the library right now studying. I'm going back to my dorm soon, but I'll be prepping well into the night. I have a huge test tomorrow morning," Julia replied.

"No problem, honey. Miss you… study hard. I know you'll do well."

"Once I'm done, I plan on watching our video and masturbating myself to sleep," Julia laughed.

"I'll be here doing the same thing," Eden chuckled back.

Julia whispers, "Why don't you call Rebecca? She would love to hook-up with you. She talks about you all the time… Or better yet, call Jordan."

"Hahaha!" Eden laughs. "Calling Jordan for a booty call is not part of my open-marriage agreement. Trust me, I'm counting down the days for you and Rebecca to get with my husband, so I can really enjoy Jordan… Every inch of him!"

"Haha… I'm looking forward to that also," Julia admitted. "Your husband is super-hot!"

"And as for Rebecca… She's cute, but right now I have a craving for this young, feisty red-head named Julia. She's got the tightest, most adorable ass on the planet… And she really fucks me hard!"

"Stop!" Julia calls out. "You're turning me on… Now I definitely need to go back to my dorm and play with myself. Then I can get my head back into these text books."

"Ditto," Eden laughs, "Love ya' babe… Miss you... I know you'll do great on your test tomorrow."

"Miss you too," Julia kisses into the phone. "We'll get together soon. I'll call you after my test and let you know how it went."

Julia ends her call and quickly packs up her belongings to exit the school library. Her vagina is totally soaked, and she can't wait to get back to her apartment to play with herself. She walks across the vast campus and sees Jordan approaching in the distance.

"Hey, handsome," she smiles.

"Hi, baby. Are you done studying?" he asked.

"No, not at all. I'm heading back to my apartment to eat something and continue studying. Are you all packed? Excited about exploring a new area?"

"Yep, I'm all packed, and just finished my last exam of the semester. I aced it!" he smiled. "Ms. Marilyn asked me to bring these files to Principal Kate. Then I'm heading out for a couple of days of relaxation and sight-seeing."

"I'm proud of you, babe," Julia replied. "You deserve it. You put a lot of effort into your studies and your grades reflect that. Now you can go away and take a couple of days to recharge without worry. I'll miss seeing you."

"Yeah... I wish you were coming with me. I'm looking forward to exploring a different part of this beautiful state that I haven't seen yet."

"I would have loved to go, but I made plans to head home and spend some quality time with my mom. You're going to love the Connecticut shoreline area. It's so quaint and beautiful. Take lots of pictures," Julia replied. "And don't forget to eat at some of the places I told you about. The seafood is incredible!"

"Haha… I will. Good luck tomorrow. I know you'll do well on your test."

He gave her a warm, comforting hug, before kissing her and continuing on his way to Principal Kate's office. After a short walk, Jordan had now arrived at Principal Kate's office. His mind quickly flashed back to the last time that he was actually in her office and how quickly their emotions took over. The way Principal Kate lost control, grabbed him, and kissed him out of nowhere, totally surprised the hell out of him. He was so in shock that she went way beyond her professional boundaries and was unable to control her emotions.

There is no denying that they both feel the chemistry and sexual tension that occurs whenever they take the time to talk, or shall we say, flirt with each other. This time none of that will happen as Jordan walks into an empty office and leaves the files on her desk, along with a cute little note that read:

"Hi Principal Kate. Sorry I missed you. I was really looking forward to seeing you. These files are from Ms. Marilyn. Have a nice day…. Jordan… Your favorite student… Lol. :)

◆ ◆ ◆

Chapter 18

It was a more than spectacular scenic drive ranging from farm lands, to back roads, to the quaint streets of the Connecticut shoreline. He passed through the beautiful towns of Guilford, Madison, Old Saybrook, Essex, and Mystic.

Being that it was a Thursday afternoon, traffic wasn't an issue, as Jordan took it all in. He stopped several times along the way to snap pictures before he arrived at a quaint bed and breakfast that was overlooking the ocean. The scenery and the amazing beauty was something that the pictures he took just couldn't capture.

The Connecticut shoreline had a vibe all its own, and it was much different from the country lifestyle of Kentville. It wasn't a bad vibe. Actually, it was really cool and just very different. People even dressed differently, with more of a preppy-style that centered around designer names, and ritzy accessories. Even their footwear, casual clothing, and jeans had a very expensive look to them. Needless to say, Jordan's mind went right to creating some hot fantasies of these well-dressed, elegant, and rich women spanking the daylights out of him.

He couldn't help but chuckle to himself as these thoughts spun circles in his crazy head. Just to think, all of these beautiful towns were less than a two-hour drive from Kentville, but yet they seemed so different. Jordan couldn't have been more excited about exploring the area and actually felt like he had been transported to another planet. There was just so much to see, discover, and, of course, taste.

After getting restaurant recommendations from the Bed and Breakfast owner, Isabella, who, by the way, was an extremely attractive, older women dressed to absolute perfection. Jordan, wrote down several of her suggestions and planned his route to explore the area.

Of course, all the while that he was talking to Isabella, Jordan was picturing himself feverishly squirming over her plush lap. He created images of himself with his underwear pulled down to his ankles, his bare bottom wiggling all over her lap, as she was administering a serious hairbrush spanking to him. Isabella, with her dark eyes and dark hair styled conservatively up in a bun, seemed to have that stern, old-fashioned, governess type of look that easily warranted these hot spanking fantasies.

He also couldn't ignore the way her eyes looked up and down at him upon checking in to her upscale Bed and Breakfast. Isabella definitely gave him a few of those slightly suspicious, squinty-eyed, stern looks that just triggered his overly active imagination. After all, it was highly uncommon for a young guy, Jordan's age, to be all by himself staying at this quaint and expensive Inn. The truth is, Jordan has the look of a male model, and anyone would think the last thing he would be is alone. Needless to say, he would most likely be masturbating tonight to these thoughts of Isabella thoroughly reddening his bare ass.

Isabella's lunch recommendation of trying several different appetizers instead of ordering a full entree was dead-on. Jordan did just that, and soon experienced the euphoria of food that the shoreline area was known for. The local fare of New England clam chowder, lobster bisque, crab cakes, and other spectacular seafood samplers was like an orgasm in his mouth. After enjoying that wonderful meal, he followed Isabella's next recommendation to taste the fresh baked desserts at a cute little local coffee shop and bakery, off the beaten path, but well-known to the town's regular customers.

Upon entry, his nose took in the heavenly smell of chocolate, cinnamon, whipped cream, sugar and everything else you can imagine as his big green eyes lit up with amazement at the pastries behind the glass counter. He couldn't resist tempting his taste buds, and ended up getting a handful of various pastries. He then carried a tray with his coffee and these delicious desserts outside to enjoy on the beautiful patio overlooking the water.

Jordan noticed several sets of eyes from customers looking at him as he walked to a table. This was not an unusual occurrence for him, as handsome as he is and having a physique that resembles a Greek God. His well-defined, horseshoe-shaped triceps and bulging biceps were definitely on display as he walked slowly and carefully carried the tray in front of him, making sure that he didn't spill his coffee. As he walked past a table of three very attractive women, their eyes shifted from staring at his muscular arms and V-shaped torso, to now focusing on his stellar lower body. So much so, that they immediately whispered something among themselves, then, one of them called out jokingly with a slight chuckle.

"You must be really trying to bulk up with a tray filled with that many calories."

Jordan literally laughed out loud at her humor as he turned his head and smiled at the beautiful woman.

"I guess it's pretty obvious that it's my first time here."

"No… Really?… You don't say?" Another of the women added, and giggled sarcastically.

Needless to say, all of their eyes were now glued to Jordan's lower body. One thing that was for sure is that he had no problem filling out his jeans as his strong athletic legs and super-toned, round ass now caught all of their attention.

Another one of the girls chimed in, and she whispered quietly among themselves, "He must have just finished doing some heavy squats and training his legs. Good God, his ass is amazing!"

The three of them chuckled to themselves as Jordan walked past them toward the available table. Just as he was about to place the tray down on top of that table next to them, the stunning woman that made the first comment stood up with a napkin in her hand and politely wiped the top of his table.

"Here, let me wipe off this table for you before you set that down. It seems that the last two idiots that sat here didn't bother cleaning up after themselves. You think they would have at least been considerate and cleaned up their crumbs and spilled coffee."

"Thank you," Jordan replied, with his pearly white smile.

"Well, my mom raised me right," she replied. "With manners and common sense."

Jordan tried his best not to overly stare at her amazing body as she continued the polite gesture of cleaning the top of the table. She was fairly tall, and beyond well-dressed, wearing a tight black and white patterned skirt that really clung to her curvy hips. Her thick muscular legs and super-plump ass were impossible to ignore as it almost poked his eyes out when she bent over to wipe his table. Her arms were also very toned, and once she had finished cleaning the tabletop, Jordan placed the tray down.

"Thanks again. That was so nice of you."

"You're welcome," she smiled.

"I'm a…" he looked at her pretty face with a slight hesitation, "I'm Jordan, by the way."

"I'm Lindsey," she added, "These are my cousins, Brittney and Katrina."

"Nice to meet you all," Jordan replied, "I was thinking you must be sisters. You all look so much alike."

"Yeah, we get that a lot," Katrina, the youngest of the cousins, added with a bit of sarcasm.

"We've definitely inherited some of the same features," Lindsey chuckled.

"Yeah, big asses," Katrina, whispered with sarcasm.

Jordan, who didn't quite hear what she said, asked, "What was that?"

"Oh nothing," Lindsey shrugged. "It's just Katrina being her obnoxious self."

Jordan smiled and added some of his humor, "It's obvious that all of you are in great shape, and you're no strangers to working out. Let me guess… It was a cheat day for the three of you also?"

His cute sense of humor made them all laugh in unison.

Brittany now chimed in with a giggle, "Not exactly. We all had salads for lunch."

"The food here is amazing. They have many healthy choices and their salads are the best. But, of course, they're known for their desserts, and as you'll soon taste, they are to die for," Lindsey added.

Jordan took the initiative to cut several of the large pastries on his tray in half. He then put them on a plate and politely passed it to them.

"Here, there's no way I'm going to eat all these goodies. I just wanted to taste as many as I could."

"Great, just what my big ass needs…. More calories," Katrina joked.

This time, Jordan clearly heard her and commented, "I don't think you three have anything to worry about. You're all stunningly beautiful, and you're all in amazing shape. It's obvious that great looks run in your family."

"Our moms are quite pretty. Katrina's mom did some modeling in her younger years. Brittney's mom did several television commercials as a teenager," Lindsey added. "My mom was a professional basketball player in the WNBA. She played for the Connecticut Sun."

Brittney quickly chimed in and pointed to her cousin, "And Lindsey here, was a professional volleyball player, and for the past several years, she's been a regional cross-fit champion."

"That explains it," Jordan smiled, as his eyes continued to take in all of Lindsey's beauty.

Lindsey quickly played it off and replied, "My cousins are very athletic too. Brittney was an amazing high school athlete. She was the star of the swim team. And Katrina ran track and was the head cheerleader in high school. So yeah, our family is quite athletic."

"Do you guys live or work here in town?" Jordan asked.

"Yep.... Live and work," Brittany added. "I'm a nurse... Well, I just graduated from nursing school. Katrina's currently in college, and Lindsey is ..."

Lindsey quickly interrupted, "I work with my mom."

Brittney took it upon herself to try to play match-maker between Jordan and her older cousin Lindsey. She quickly volunteered more of Lindsey's achievements.

"She not only works with her mom, she's a complete bad-ass! She owns a couple of buildings, including the massive Templeton building. It has a state-of-the-art fitness center, a couple of restaurants, some retail stores, and several medical offices in it."

Lindsey quickly shifted the focus off herself and asked, "So how about you, Jordan... Um... Last name?... What brings you here?"

"Thompson," Jordan replied with a slight chuckle. "Jordan Thompson... I'm on break for a week. I go to The Academy, a private college in Kentville."

"The Academy?" Lindsey smirked and added, "You seem older. I thought you were my age."

"Age doesn't matter when your hot as fuck," Katrina chimed in. "Right Lindsey?"

Lindsey flashed Katrina a stern, scowling look, they instantly made her younger cousin bury her head into her cell phone and feverishly type away.

"I am a bit older and not the typical age of a first year college student," Jordan smirked and explained. "Just a number of unplanned events led me to attend The Academy."

"I can't find him on any social media," Katrina blurted out.

Her eyes then looked at both of her cousins, before she gave Jordan an overly suspicious, skeptical look.

Chapter 19

Jordan took a deep breath and quickly addressed her concern,

"Ever since I was a victim of identity theft last year, I deleted all of my social media accounts," he answered. "Thankfully, I got back all the money that was stolen from my account. That's why I'm not doing any social media. I also deleted any Apps from my phone that accessed my bank information."

"See!" Lindsey quickly chimed in, "That's exactly what I've done. I haven't logged onto my social media accounts in years… And no way in hell will I allow any of my kids to be on any of them."

Lindsey then turned to her two cousins, "I've been telling you guys. Be careful with all those crazy phone apps. Use cash and stop charging everything!"

Brittney looked at Jordan, feeling a bit awkward that she judged him for a moment over his lack of social media presence. She quickly complimented him.

"Well, you are obviously brilliant and also a very gifted athlete to get into that school," she mentioned. "You know, Lindsey almost went there."

"Really?" Jordan responded.

"Yeah… That was years ago," Lindsey paused for a moment

before answering, "I was on the pro volleyball circuit, and I was fortunate to make enough money, especially from several endorsement deals, to pay for it. I was going to attend college at The Academy once the volleyball championships were over. I even met with the owner and Principal Marilyn. She actually offered me a scholarship. It wouldn't have cost me a dime!"

"Wow! We have that in common," Jordan announced. "Ms. Marilyn granted me a scholarship! I would never be able to afford tuition."

"You're kidding…." Lindsey humorously responded. "Shut the front door."

"Here she is!" Katrina then pulled up an article on her phone that featured Lindsey in action as a volleyball player.

Katrina held her phone up, scrolled through and showed Jordan a number of pictures of her cousin, Lindsey, in action as a pro athlete.

"Great! Just what I wanted," Lindsey sarcastically shook her head at Katrina. "To have a complete stranger see pictures of me in my bathing suit playing volleyball."

"Oooops," Katrina laughed. "We're just proud of you, Linds… Take a chill pill."

"It looked like you had an amazing career!" Jordan really perked-up. "By the way, Marilyn and Marjorie are still the owners of the school, but Principal Kate runs the day-to-day operations."

"I'm sure it's still an amazing school," Lindsey replied.

"It's phenomenal," Jordan smiled. "If you don't mind me asking… What was the reason that you chose not to go?"

"It was winter, my volleyball circuit was over, and I was all set to start school in the fall," Lindsey chuckled, "Then, to my surprise… Whammo!… my daughter happened."

Lindsey giggled and continued explaining, "From that point on, it was all about raising her. Plus, I knew that I wanted to have more children."

"That's understandable," Jordan smiled. "I bet you're an amazing mom."

"She's more than amazing! She's the best mom ever!" Brittany added. "Her kids are awesome and so polite."

"I try," Lindsey smiled.

"Oh, come on, Lindsey," Katrina now jumped into the conversation. "She's a fucking super-woman! Not only is she the world's most amazing mom, but she also built a number of very successful businesses. She still has several high-end clients that she personally trains and even does nutrition for them. Add to that, she now co-owns a thriving business with her mom."

Brittany chimed in, "Let's not forget that she wrote a top-selling fitness and nutrition book aimed at women that are pregnant."

"Here it is!" Katrina, again used her phone to pull up Lindsey's book, along with another featured article about her.

"Wow! Lindsey Templeton, a New York Times bestseller!" Jordan replied.

"Okay, guys," Lindsey tried to shrug off her accomplishments. "This isn't the Lindsey Templeton show."

"YEP!" Jordan chuckled, and smiled at Lindsey. "I'd say that qualifies you for Wonder Woman status!"

"About the only thing she did wrong was marry her husband… Mr. Dick Head!" Katrina added.

"Ex-husband," Brittney quickly added. "Lying, cheating, looser!"

"Total ASSHOLE!" Katrina added.

"Okay, okay, you two!" Lindsey stopped them, "Watch that mouth of yours, Katrina. And let's not forget that he is still the father to my kids, and despite being a horrible husband, he is an amazing dad."

"He's still a fucking asshole dick head in my eyes," Katrina blurted out again.

"Kat!" Lindsey, gave her a super-disapproving look, "Your mouth! That woman sitting a couple of tables over from us has two young kids. Geez!"

Lindsey was now extremely annoyed with her younger cousin, Katrina, "There's a time and a place for language like that. It's not out in public with young kids nearby."

"They didn't hear me," Katrina rolled her eyes.

"You were pretty loud, Kat," Brittney added. "The lady definitely heard you. She looked over at you… At all of us!"

"Since you guys live here, what do you recommend I see and do?" Jordan asked.

"So much," Lindsey replied. "Canoe or paddle board the Connecticut river, shop at the outlets, there are some great museums, boat tours, the casino's are a must."

"Mystic Pizza!" Katrina added. "Have you ever seen the Julia Roberts movie? The one that really started her career?"

"No, I haven't," Jordan replied.

"It was filmed here years ago," Lindsey added. "It really made our tourism boom, especially in the summer months. Even so, we have a lot of amazing restaurants, and some great pizza."

"I'm here for a week," Jordan added. "I'll make sure to try it."

"Lindsey, you love that place. You should take him there and show him around the area," Brittney, once again, tried to set them up for a date.

"I would love that!" Jordan replied, "No pressure, of course, as it sounds like you're a busy mom, with a demanding work schedule."

"Um…" Lindsey stumbled. "I'm not really into dating someone that's just wondering through town."

"Come on, Lindsey," Brittney now added. "I mean look at him… He's really polite, cute, and seems down-to-earth."

"He's hot as hell!" Katrina added.

Brittney quickly interrupted, "Show him around. Have dinner, go to the casino's... Kat and I will even babysit if you need us to."

"Maybe we can do something active, like I mentioned," Lindsey smiled, "Canoe or paddle board, then, have lunch."

Katrina, with her wise mouth, blurted out to Lindsey in a low voice, "I'd do something much more active with him! I'd fuck his brains out, especially with a body like that!"

Katrina's intention was to only have Lindsey hear that comment, but unfortunately, her whisper was a bit too loud, and still audible to Jordan and Brittney.

"Kat!" Lindsey scowled at her younger cousin.

Jordan's handsome face actually blushed with redness, as he smiled and tilted his head downward.

"You'll have to excuse my younger cousin, Katrina," Lindsey apologized. "It's her first day out of the insane asylum. She's still learning how to speak and interact with others."

"Hahaha!" Jordan, along with Brittney, erupted with laughter.

"Very funny!" Katrina, sardonically rolled her eyes at Lindsey.

Lindsey now really scowled at Katrina with furrowed eyebrows.

"I'm literally about two seconds away from kicking your butt, Katrina. You're about to have a size 8 shoe sticking out of your plump rear-end for all to see!"

Katrina's face filled with fear as she quickly retreated and apologized, "Sorry, Linds."

"I've warned you before about your mouth," Lindsey reminded her. "Remember the day when you were swearing up a storm around my kids?… You're lucky you still have your teeth!"

Brittney stepped in and added some humor to try and defuse the situation.

"Kat, you have the best teeth of all us… So I would chill if I were you."

"Now, as for you, my sexy older cousin… Stop over-analyzing," Brittney now encouraged Lindsey. "You and Jordan have so much in common. He's in The Academy, he's brilliant, totally into fitness, loves to sight see, and he even thinks like you regarding social media and phone apps."

Katrina quickly added, "He's obviously not one of those local, spoon-fed, trust-fund, never-worked-a-day in their life, wealthy guys, that got everything handed to them. He's really cool!"

Katrina, went on with her jokes, "And his name isn't Biff, and he's not wearing a watch that costs more than my car!"

"Geez, Thanks…" Jordan giggled at Katrina's comment.

"Okay, where are you staying, Jordan?" Lindsey asked him.

"I'm at the INN on riverside," he replied.

"Oh, Isabella's place?"

"Yep!" Jordan nodded.

"Okay, here… put your number into my phone." Lindsey handed her cell phone to him.

"I'm working tomorrow. Unfortunately, I'm tied up on Saturday because I'm having a yard sale... But I'm totally free on Sunday," Lindsey replied.

She then texted him her phone number as his phone chimed with a message alert.

"That's my cell number," she smiled at him.

"Hey, he should come by the yard sale. With those muscles, he can definitely help carry some of the big furniture items out on the lawn," Brittney added.

"I would be more than willing to help you," Jordan smiled.

"Why don't you guys go out to dinner after your yard sale?" Katrina added.

"I'll tell you what..." Lindsey responded, "I'll reserve some paddle-boards for Sunday, and we'll go out on the river, then out for lunch. We don't need help setting things up, but come by the yard sale tomorrow afternoon. We should be done at about 4pm. Then, we'll play it by ear. My ex has the kids, so I'm free. We'll go out and get something to eat."

"Shit!... She sure has a lot of self-control," Katrina joked. "I'd be hitting you up for a booty-call tonight if I was her."

"You're really funny, Katrina," Jordan giggled.

"She's really annoying... That's what she is!" Lindsey shot

Katrina a more than stern look. "And very immature… 22 going on 12!"

Jordan couldn't help but smile to himself as he took in another view of just how absolutely stunning Lindsey was, the moment she stood up from the table. Her slightly sun-kissed skin, long blonde hair that blew perfectly in the wind, all blended together with a physique that literally could stop traffic.

Lindsey, along with her two younger cousins, all gave Jordan a friendly hug.

"Thanks for the desserts," Brittney chimed. "That was really classy of you."

"Yeah… my big butt thanks you for giving me more calories," Katrina added with her wit.

"You guys are welcome," Jordan chuckled. "I enjoyed talking to you."

Lindsey stuck around for a moment after her two younger cousins walked away.

"Hey handsome," she smiled at him, "I'm sorry I have my guard up. It's been a while since I've met anyone that I even wanted to get to know better. And being a mom, I'm super careful who I get involved with, for my kids sake."

"Like I said… I can just tell that you're an amazing mom," he replied.

"I'm a busy mom," Lindsey joked. "Between working with my mom and my three monkeys, I'm pretty busy!"

"They must be as cute as can be," Jordan chuckled, "Like you."

"You're really making it hard for me to resist you, Jordan Thompson," she hugged him tightly. "Damn! And you smell so good!"

He smiled. "I'm so glad I met you, Lindsey Templeton. I will let you take the lead. The ball is in your court… call me."

"You know it's dangerous giving an ex-volleyball player like me the ball. I might just spike it!" Lindsey joked.

Jordan didn't say anything, but just flashed her his beautiful, boyish smile before they walked away.

"Hey Jordan, I'll call you tonight. It won't be for a booty call," Lindsey laughed, "Maybe we'll just meet up for a glass of wine and talk."

"Sounds good," Jordan confirmed, and watched her walk away.

It was very obvious that one of the things the girls all inherited was amazing genetics. Even though the girls ranged in height from Katrina and Brittney being about 5'4 or 5'5, to Lindsey standing about 5'8 or 5'9, they all had the same features. They were all blonde, beyond beautiful with curvy hips, strong, thick legs, and super-plump, totally round, rear-ends.

As beautiful as all three of them were, there was no doubt that Jordan was totally fixated on Lindsey. There was something about her that actually reminded him of Principal Kate. After all, from what he gathered, she was about the same age, and a super-mom, as well. Plus, she was once a pro-athlete and still kept herself in amazing shape.

He took his last sip of coffee, before packing up some of the desserts that he didn't even get to eat. He got into his car and headed off, ready to see more of this beautiful area. That night, he met with Lindsey for a quick drink before she had to get back and tuck her kids into bed. She also had a full day of work on Friday, so they only met for a little over an hour. Even so, it was more than obvious that they were drawn to each other, and the conversation between them flowed effortlessly.

Lindsey, purposely kept so much about her life now, with her three kids, and working with her mom, out of their conversation. Instead, she focused on talking about fun-stuff, like food, travel and exercise. She also was very interested in hearing what Jordan's passions and goals are. Since she was already skeptical of dating when the topic of relationships came up, Jordan made it clear about his current status.

He filled Lindsey in on everything regarding his life in college, working, and attending The Academy. He even talked briefly about Julia, and made it perfectly clear that right now, he's just dating and chooses to be in non-exclusive relationship. Of course, he didn't come out and tell Lindsey all about his kinky nature, his fetish and spanking interests, the affair he's having with Nurse Madison, or any of the recent threesomes that recently blew his mind. He wisely kept all that to himself, especially, since he didn't want to scare her away during this get-to-know each other phase.

Lindsey and Jordan ended their conversation on Thursday night with a warm hug, and made plans to meet up after her yard sale, late afternoon, on Saturday. Needless to say, even though he remained tight-lipped about all of his kinky interests, he couldn't help but fantasize about her. The truth was, he masturbated twice that night with the images of him doing everything under the sun to Lindsey, and having her do it all right back to him.

Chapter 20

It's a warm, slightly overcast, Friday morning as the sun is trying to peak through a small layer of clouds in the quaint New England town by the shore. It was the usual morning chaos at the Templeton household with family members scattered in all directions, like leaves blowing in the wind.

Jessica Templeton, who is Karina's mom, was running her usual morning marathon of getting her two teenagers ready for school, as well as trying to get herself together for work. She's in the kitchen, scouring through the refrigerator, looking for food items to pack for their lunches. Still wrapped in a towel, with her blonde shoulder-length hair, damp as can be, she manages to take a quick sip of her morning coffee.

"Yuck!" she replies and spits out the now cold liquid into the kitchen sink.

"Dammit!… I have nothing to pack for them," she mumbles, "She was supposed to go grocery shopping yesterday."

"Katrina, I need help down here getting your brother and sister's lunches together," she called out to her oldest daughter.

Just then her phone rang. Jessica glances at it and sees it's her twin sister, Jeanine, on the call display.

"Hey sis," she answered in a hurried tone, "What's up?"

"Hey, you okay?… You sound frazzled."

"I am," Jessica replied, "The usual... I'm running around like crazy here."

"Same here," Jeanine replied in a similar type of huff, "That's why I'm calling. I want your opinion. I'm thinking about calling Paula and hiring her to help me with Brittney."

"Really?… Why?" Jessica replied, "She's just going to say that she told you so. You know how sis is."

"Well, maybe she was right all along," Jeanine answered, "I should've laid down the law a long time ago and been a spanking mom. I don't know about you, and your kids, but I know that my daughter definitely can use some serious discipline… Her attitude, her actions, you name it."

Jeanine continues to rant, "I mean, she's 25 and a nurse for God's sake. She shouldn't be out drinking and spending money like it's going out of style. She keeps buying a ton of clothes, isn't home much, and doesn't help me with the chores around here. If that's the case, she should move out and get her own place. Then she'll realize how expensive everything is. The mortgage, the heating bills, home insurance…"

Jessica interrupted her, "I hear you. I'm having the same issue with Katrina… Hold on, Jen."

Jessica covers the phone and yells up the stairs to her daughter.

"Katrina, there are no groceries here... Did you go grocery shopping yesterday?"

There's no answer from her oldest child, which forces her to yell even louder.

"Katrina!... Do you hear me?" Jessica's voice now really escalated.

"Sorry, Jeanine," she went back to her conversation with her sister.

"So, you want sis to spank Brittney?" Jessica asked her.

"Well, that's what she does for a living," Jeanine responded, "Lord knows, her business is thriving because of non-spanking moms like us, that are way too lenient with their kids. She even made Lindsey a full-on partner."

"Yeah, Paula told me that," Jessica acknowledged, "She said that Lindsey is an even harder spanker than she is. I mean, can you imagine being spanked by Lindsey? As physically fit and as strong as she is. Still competing and winning cross-fit and weight lifting competitions... at age 33? That's insane!"

Jeanine added, "And don't forget, Lindsey was a spanking mom right from the start. Her three kids are freaking angels. After all, she learned it from her mom."

"That she did," Jessica replied. "I remember seeing her as a teenager getting spanked by sis. Lindsey had the cutest, tightest rear-end on the planet."

"She still does," Jeanine replied, "Only now it's even bigger, more round, and still as toned as can be. The other day when I saw her in the gym, it looked like she had two melons underneath her black leggings. She had every guy and girl starring at her ass in admiration."

Jessica chuckled at Jeanine's comment, "It runs in the family, sis. We've all been blessed with those genetics… Or cursed, whatever way you want to look at it. My rear-end looks like a giant pumpkin!"

"Hahaha!" Jeanine laughed at her sister's humor. "Mine too, sis… Ain't that the truth!"

She then continued, "Jess, that fact is that Paula was constantly on her daughter's butt throughout her school years. Don't you remember? It seemed every time we visited sis, and went over to her house, she had Lindsey's cute volleyball-shaped bare bottom perched over her knee, getting a dose of the hairbrush."

Jessica, now reminded of those times and images, chuckled, "She never held back and she didn't care who was there watching."

Jeanine agreed, "Exactly! If Lindsey misbehaved, sis would yank her panties down in a heartbeat and redden her bottom until she cried a river!"

"I've seen that happen so much that I lost count," Jessica giggled.

Just then, Jessica's middle child, Melissa, the super-cute 16-year-old athletic student, called out to her from upstairs.

"Hey mom, I can't find my practice shirt."
"And where are my new jeans?" she adds in a semi-mumbled tone as she brushes her teeth.

Jessica turned her attention back to her phone conversation with Jeanine, "I hate to admit it, but I think you're right. I'm beyond frustrated with Katrina. Ever since the divorce, she's been totally slacking off and not doing her chores around here. Even though her dad and I never spanked her, she would at least listen to him. I think we should hire both Paula and Lindsey to get our daughters back on track."

"You know we will have to swallow our pride," Jeanine reminded her.

"Yeah, I can hear her now. She's going to remind us how much mom spoiled us for being the youngest," Jessica joked, "Paula's going to go on and on about how mom spanked her so much more than us because she was the oldest and had to set an example."

"Well, she is right, sis," Jeanine admitted, "That was true. You and I got spanked on occasion when we really misbehaved, but mom really tanned Paula's plump bottom all throughout her teenage years. She didn't let her get away with anything."

Jessica gets interrupted again as her youngest child, Ryan, calls down from upstairs.

"Hey Mom, do we have any extra tubes of toothpaste?"

"I need it for the science project and I put it on the grocery list," he added.

"One minute, sweetheart," Jessica answered her son, "I'll be right up. I'm on the phone with Aunty Jeanine."

"Okay, Jeanine, I agree," Jessica stated. "I think it's time for Brittney and Katrina to get their first spanking. It will set them straight and in the right direction. I'll stop over at Paula's office and see what she suggests. Then, I'll call you later."

"K, sis… Luv u."

"Love you, too," Jessica ended the call and focused her attention back on her chaotic household.

Chapter 21

Jessica took a moment to breathe deeply before letting it out.

"So much for going to gym," she says to herself, and runs back up the flight of stairs to the second level of her house.

It's literally been the third time she jogged up those stairs in the last 4 minutes. She knocks on the bedroom door of her oldest daughter.

"Katrina, wake up! You have chores to help me with," she speaks into the closed door of Katrina's bedroom.

"She probably has her earbuds in, mom," Ryan, her beyond brilliant 14-year-old son, announced.

"Mom… The toothpaste?" he asked, "Remember?… My Science project?"

The super-stressed mom shakes her head in frustration, "Go into the front pocket of my gym bag, honey. I should have a tube in there. You can take it."

"Thanks mom," Ryan smiled, "Don't worry about my lunch. I'll use my allowance money and buy it."

"Don't buy junk food, Ryan," his mom replied back.

"I can do the same, mom," Melissa responded, "Pizza isn't junk food. Think about it... It has protein from the meat and cheese, carbs from the dough, and mushrooms, peppers, olives. All the food groups."

Her humor breaks the tension as Jessica, still wrapped in a towel, now looks through the laundry basket.

"Shit!" she swears, as she pulls out Melissa's dirty practice jersey from the basket.

"Oooh," Ryan giggles, "You're not supposed to swear, mom. Put a dollar in the jar downstairs."

"In that case, I'll put a five," His mom replies with four more swears, "Shit, shit, shit, shit!"

"Your practice jersey is in the laundry," she now yells downstairs to Melissa, who's rummaging through the downstairs clothing bin, looking for her new jeans.

"It's cool mom," Melissa calls out to her, "I'll wear a sports top... Found them!"

"Found what?" Jessica asks.

"My new jeans, silly," Melissa replied, "They're clean but, of course, Katrina didn't fold the laundry.

Just then, Katrina, her oldest daughter, emerges from the bedroom. Even with her long blonde hair all knotted up like a birds nest, the 22-year-old is about as stunning as can be. Her big brown eyes opened wide to watch her mom, still wrapped in a bath towel, scrambling like a chicken with its head cut off.

"Nice of you to join us, Missy!" Jessica scowled at her oldest child.

"Yeah, well, I was exhausted," Katrina scowled back at her mom.

"Join the club!" Her mom replied in a huff. "You didn't go grocery shopping yesterday. You didn't fold and bring up the laundry. What the hell, Kat?"

"That's six dollars, mom," Ryan smirked as he headed downstairs.

"Mom, you need to sign our report cards," Melissa called up to her.

"I'll sign it for them," Katrina replied, as she walked down stairs and headed straight to the coffee pot.

"Uh!… No you won't. I'll be right down."

Once again, the pretty mom jogged back down the stairs and entered the kitchen. She took the pen out of Katrina's hand and attempted to sign Melissa's and Ryan's report cards. Just her luck, the pen didn't write, so she rushed over to the utility drawer to get another pen.

"Where the hell are all the pens?" she called out as she fumbled through the junk-filled drawer.

"Mom..." Ryan reminded her.

"I know Ryan," she shook her head, "Sometimes you just need to swear!"

"Fuck yeah," Katrina quickly replied.

"Whoa! A dollar in the jar," Ryan reminded his sister.

"Yeah right, brain-head," she smirked at him, "I barely got any tips at work last night."

"Using the F-word was uncalled for, Katrina!"

Jessica scolded her daughter as she continued to search for a pen that would actually write. Unable to find one, she quickly walked in the direction of the living room closet.

"Uh!... I'll get a pen from my purse," she replied.

As she turned and walked hastily with a purpose into the living room, the towel wrapped around her body fell to the floor. A round of giggles immediately came out of each of her kids mouths as she found herself stark naked and fully exposed. She quickly put one hand over her vagina and the other over her breast, as she turned away. Of course, this left her super-plump, more than ample, rear-end in full view.

"Cover your eyes, and turn away, Ryan," she immediately called out to her son in embarrassment.

"Nice booty, mom," Katrina sarcastically commented, "See… running up and down the stairs is doing wonders for your glutes!… Who needs the gym?"

"Yeah, nice hiney, mom," Ryan now giggled with his back turned.

"Zip it, both of you!" she now squinted her eyes at Katrina. "Once again, you didn't get your chores done and I'm running around like a mad woman!"

Melissa picked up the towel and walked it over to her mom in the living room. With Ryan turned away and facing the wall, Jessica didn't even bother reaching for it as she fumbled inside her purse for a pen. Thankfully, this time she found one that worked, and quickly signed her kids report cards.

"Here, give this to Ryan and hurry, before you miss the bus," she traded the signed report cards for the towel.

As Melissa and Ryan left the house, Jessica wrapped the towel back over her body. Absolutely furious, she really scolded her daughter.

"This needs to stop, young lady. You are 22-years-old and I need help around here. I don't ask you for much!" Her voice now really escalated at Katrina.

"Your dad and I cover all your bills… Your car, your insurance, your phone, not to mention your freaking college!"

Katrina froze for a moment, completely stunned and not used to hearing her mom yell at her like that. She knew her mom was right and that she was often lackadaisical and flat-out lazy at times. She's taken a semester off from college to figure out her career path and next move. She's been trying to find a better job since working part-time as a waitress. She refrained from saying anything as her mom was still on a rant.

"I really need your help around here, Katrina. Grocery shopping, laundry, cleaning, lunches, it all needs to be done. Ryan and Melissa are doing their part and I need you to step up and do the same!"

Her mom's tone said it all as she continued, "Fuck! Times like this, I miss your dad. I miss the little things he did and how much he helped me with the three of you."

"I'll do better, mom," Katrina replied, "I know I've been slacking off. I've been trying to find a better job and wondering what my next move is. I really don't know what I want to do… The only thing I'm really interested in is fitness."

"Then get certified and teach classes or start personal training. With a body like yours, you'll make a killing," Her mom complimented her. "Talk to your cousin, Lindsey. She did that for years, and I think she still trains a few select clients… For a lot of money!"

"Yeah, I'll ask her," Katrina replied, "She's having a yard sale tomorrow and I offered to help her. Of course, I want first dibs on her clothing. She's actually bringing some of her old jeans and clothes over here tonight for me and Brittney to have. I can't wait!"

"Hmm…" Jessica couldn't help but smirk to herself, "Did you say that Lindsey is coming over here tonight?"

"Yep, us cousins are getting together," Katrina replied. "Brittney's coming over also."

Jessica's silent smirk continued for a few more seconds as her recent conversation with Jeanine resonated within her.

With no one else but Katrina home, she now tugged off the towel and walked into the bathroom to get ready for work. Katrina couldn't help but chuckle at the full view of her moms plump over-sized bare bottom walking down the hallway and into the bathroom. It literally bounced up and down like a super-inflated basketball, jiggling with each step she took. Of course, the sight of her mom's big bouncy booty made it even easier for Katrina to unleash another one of her quirky jokes.

"Hey mom?" Katrina called out.

"What is it Kat?" Jessica, now very annoyed, stopped in her

tracks and turned to her daughter. "I'm late and I have got to get going."

She stood there completely naked and waited for her daughter to answer. Katrina did a stellar job of hiding her laughter long enough to deliver.

"You know, mom, if you go to McDonald's or Burger King on the way to work, you can order some fries to go with that shake of yours."

"Haha, very funny, Katrina," her mom replied in a less than impressed sarcastic voice.

"People who live in glass houses shouldn't throw stones," she joked back at her daughter. "That butt of yours is going to be just as big, if not bigger than mine. It already looks like an over-inflated balloon."

"Haha," Katrina laughed, "That was a good one, mom."

She then continued into the bathroom to put her make-up on and style her hair. Thankfully, there was now a calm, peaceful vibe in her house. It was just like every other weekday morning in Jessica Templeton's chaotic household. However, once her two teenagers go off to school, the morning stress eases up a bit.

It hasn't been an easy two years for the pretty mom since she ended her 23-year marriage to David, the dad to her children. It sure was nice having a man around the house to get things done and keep the kids focused and on-track.

David was and still is a great dad, and continues to be a wonderful provider. In fact, he and Jessica share joint custody of Ryan and Melissa, and both teenagers have adapted incredibly well to splitting their time between each of their parents houses.

Jessica would be the first to admit that their love had faded and they were just going through the motions as husband and wife. Perhaps, if it wasn't for David's cheating ways, they might still have been married. However, what's done is done and now Jessica runs her household, works full-time, and still manages to stay active and fairly well in shape.

The truth is, the 5 foot 5, 47 year-old, curvy bombshell still draws stares from every direction, especially with that perfectly plump ass of hers. The pretty mom finishes getting dressed, gives her stylish blonde hair one more blast of hairspray, dabs on some perfume, and heads for the door.

"Katrina, I'm leaving," she calls out, "Make sure you go grocery shopping, fold the laundry, and start another load of wash. I want all these clothes completely clean and put away by the time I come home. Is that clear?"

"Whatever, mom," Katrina responds in an irritated tone, then retreats back to her bedroom.

Chapter 22

Jessica, now only a few minutes from work, sends a quick text message to her employee stating that she's going to be a bit late today. She now deviates to a crossing street and proceeds down that road to where Paula's office is located. She pulls into the parking lot and smiles as she looks up at the huge sign out front, with big bold lettering identifying the business, "**Crimson Bottoms – Discipline Services For Families**". Another sign underneath it stresses by appointment only, and displays the company's phone number.

Jessica gets out of her car and proceeds to ring the doorbell of the building. As she looks up, she notices the video camera following her every move. Two seconds later, Lindsey's voice comes over the loud speaker attached to the side of the doorway.

"Aunty Jess! What a nice surprise!" she says excitedly, "I'm on the phone, but I'll buzz you in."

After the door unlocks with the annoying sound of a buzzer, Jessica proceeds up the stairs into the main waiting area. Lindsey, who is currently on a phone call, waves to her, then motions with her index finger to hold on.

Jessica smiles at her and can't help but tune-in to the conversation as Lindsey addresses the questions of the potential customer.

"Yes, Ma'am. I'm Lindsey Templeton," Lindsey replied to the caller. "I'll have to thank them for the referral. How can I help you?"

Lindsey listens, then responds to the caller, "Yes, I totally understand. I have three kids of my own and when they misbehave, their bottoms get profusely spanked."

"It's okay, Ma'am," she continued, "Many moms are like you. They are not strict disciplinarians or spanking moms. I am, and so is my mom, Paula. That is what we specialize in here."

Lindsey smirked at her aunt, waiting patiently, as the caller continued to ask a series of questions. Being the adamant professional that she is, Lindsey listened intently to the woman's concerns.

"Yes, Ma'am... Absolutely. If your daughter is that defiant, then I suggest you take action. Sometimes there's no other way than with a good old-fashioned bare bottom spanking."

Lindsey continued, "Yes, Ma'am... I can either come to your location for an extra fee, or you can bring your child here to our office. That's totally up to you, Ma'am. If you would like to be present and in the room when I discipline your child, you are more than welcome. You'll see first hand how I spank and paddle a bare bottom... And if needed, my leather strap will come out as well. That's what I use on my own kids to adjust their attitude and behavior."

Lindsey shrugged her shoulders and then sent another pretty smile to her Aunt Jessica as she continued to finalize the details with the customer.

"Sure Ma'am... Name?... Ms. Roberts... Your child's name and age?... Suzanne, 17... Let me check the schedule. How is 1pm?... Great!"

Lindsey continued, "For sure, Ms. Roberts... I totally understand. That usually happens the moment they see our building and the sign. No worries, I'll be downstairs a few minutes earlier in the doorway waiting for you."

With the call just about ending, Lindsey gives one final reassurance.

"Well, Ma'am, I can assure you that if Suzanne tries to run, she won't get far before I catch her... I promise you Ms. Roberts, when I'm done with your daughter's bottom, she won't be sitting comfortably for a few days... Okay, see ya' at 1."

Lindsey finally ends the call and now stands up to properly greet her Aunt Jessica. She's a totally stunning, curvaceous woman with long wavy blonde hair and big emerald green eyes. The moment she opens her arms to give Jessica a hug, her super-toned biceps literally pop out like boulders with incredible muscle definition. Her entire physique is impeccable as her curvy hips flow down from a narrow waistline like a winding country road. Her thighs are rock-solid and thick with well-defined muscle tone. And the truth is, her ass is the most talked about thing in town! It's totally plump, as round as planet earth, and exquisite beyond belief. It protrudes out like a basketball and makes her tight green skirt look like a hot air balloon over it. This forces Lindsey to constantly adjust and pull her skirt downward to prevent it from riding up her luscious hips.

There is no denying that Lindsey is a bad-ass woman. At age 33, mom of three kids, and a cross-fit champion, she is someone that can hold her own with just about anyone. Standing 5 foot 9, with impeccable posture, Lindsey just commands attention. She now embraces her aunt with a warm, loving hug.

"It's great to see you, Aunty Jess," Lindsey greeted her. "My God, you look stunning!… That outfit is killer!"

Jessica smiles from ear to ear hearing that from Lindsey, who looks breath-takingly beautiful and is one of the most stylish women she knows.

"And look at you!… You get more beautiful everytime I see you," Jessica replied. "And I see that you're back to using your maiden name."

"There was no freaking way that I was going to keep using my ex-husband's last name," Lindsey strongly stated. "I'm a Templeton through and through."

"Yes you are!… And you are a strong, independent woman, and an amazing mom. I'm so proud of you," Jessica complimented her niece. "And girl... that body of yours must stop traffic!"

Lindsey laughed, "Well, I sure inherited the plump Templeton ass. Just like my mom, you, Aunty Jeanine, even your kids and my kids have it!"

"Yeah, but yours looks like a basketball. It's so tight and lifted," Jessica chuckles, "Mine looks like an oversized pumpkin!"

"Hahaha!… Come in… Sit down, sit down, Aunty Jess. Mom is in a discipline session down the hall," Lindsey announces, "A frustrated mom brought in her two kids because they constantly fight with each other."

"Ah!… I see," Jessica nodded, "Two boys?"

"No… Actually a brother and sister, 17 and 15 years-old," Lindsey replied.

It was unusually quiet in the office, and Jessica was expecting to hear all the spanking action that was happening down the hallway. She inconspicuously tried to listen, and was barely able to hear the ever so faint sounds of slaps and cries coming from the room at the very end of the hallway.

"We just had new sound proofing installed in our two discipline rooms," Lindsey volunteered. "You won't hear much more than those muffled sounds."

"Usually, we don't even hear a peep from those rooms," Lindsey chuckled and continued, "My mom must be giving it to them good. I'm willing to bet those kids are crying their eyes out and yelping like crazy."

Lindsey's humor makes Jessica flat-out laugh out loud. Just then, the office phone rang and Lindsey signaled to Jessica to hold on for a second. She walked over to the phone on top of her desk and answered the call with a very professional and pleasant tone.

"Crimson Bottoms, Family Discipline Services. This is Lindsey Templeton. How can I help you?"

Jessica couldn't hear the questions that were being asked by the caller, but Lindsey was forthcoming enough that it didn't matter.

"Yes, Ma'am, exactly..." Lindsey replied to the caller, "The discipline is administered by either my mom or me, and in some cases, if needed, both of us together."

After fielding another series of questions, Lindsey responded to the caller.

"Yes, Ma'am, that is correct. Our spankings are always given on the bare bottom and we will have a private consultation with you prior. We will thoroughly discuss the problem, the severity, and so forth... Sure, I will schedule you in for Monday at 3pm for a consult. Please go to our website and fill out the proper forms. Have a nice day and I'll see you on Monday, at 3."

The moment that phone call ended, another call came in. Once again, Lindsey motioned to her Aunt, then chuckled, "Uh!... Hold on Aunty Jess. It's been a busy morning."

She proceeded to answer that call.

"Crimson Bottoms, Discipline Services. This is Lindsey Templeton. How can I help you?"

That call ended quickly with Lindsey addressing the company's policy.

"No Sir. I'm sorry we do not spank individual males. I suggest you try a Dominatrix. Our focus is to help families. Have a nice day."

Jessica immediately laughed, "You must get a lot of those calls."

"Actually, not many," Lindsey replied. "We stress family discipline services, so it's kind of understood. However, we recently expanded and we will now discipline single guys and girls if they are between the ages of 21-30 years-old. They have to be currently enrolled in college or have been given a written notice by their employer for disciplinary actions. Our lawyers have even drafted a standard form for the HR departments of companies that want to hire us."

"Wow!" Jessica replied, "What a great idea! I'll have to remember that before I fire an employee."

Lindsey acknowledged, "It could be their last chance before you terminate them."

"I bet you came up with that, and not my stuffy sister. Am I right?" Jessica asked.

"Yeah, that was my idea," Lindsey smiled. "I have one other idea that I'm talking to our lawyers about. I want to expand and accept husbands, wives, any partners that are legally married. They have to come in as a couple, and of course, sign our waiver forms."

Lindsey continued with excitement, "Think about it, Aunty Jess. It could help a marriage to hold each other accountable. Maybe there will be fewer cases of divorce… I don't know. It's just a thought. I'm still working on the details."

"I love it!" Jessica responded to her niece. "I think it's brilliant. Especially if one of them spends too much money, doesn't pull their weight, or they argue about stupid things. They could resolve their differences by having a third party like you and your mom discipline them. What an amazing idea!"

"Well, let's keep that between us," Lindsey smirked. "I haven't even mentioned that idea to my mom."

"Done! It's our secret," Jessica replied, "Your mom did the right thing by making you a partner. You have brilliant ideas and I hate to say this, but I'm willing to bet that you are an even harder spanker than she is."

"Haha!" Lindsey laughed out loud, "Even though my mom is well past her prime, she can still deliver one hell of a spanking… but yes, she passes all the problem cases over to me. I get to handle all the really feisty ones. The ones that struggle, resist, talk back, and so on."

"So… speaking of feisty," Jessica took a deep breath and continued, "The reason I'm here is because I want to actually hire you and my sister."

"Hire me and mom?" Lindsey asked with a more than surprised tone.

"Actually, Aunty Jeanine and I want to hire you and your mom to spank Brittney and Katrina," Jessica continued.

"Both of us are at our wits end with our daughters. They are disrespectful, still living at home, spending way too much money, and not doing their share of the work in our households."

"Hmmm," Lindsey nodded and listened as Jessica continued.

"Aunt Jeanine and I admit that we let our kids get away with way too much growing up. God, I hate to say this, but your mom was right all along. We should have laid down the law and spanked them early on whenever they misbehaved. Instead, we tried to talk to them, reason with them, take away their toys and phones."

"You can talk and try all that reasoning stuff as much as possible," Lindsey interrupted, "But nothing works better than an old-fashioned bare bottom spanking… Just ask my kids!"

Jessica chuckled at Lindsey's response, "I can just hear your mom already."

She then changed her voice to imitate her sister Paula's, "Jessica, I told you so. You never wanted to listen to me… Spare the rod, spoil the child… Finally, you've come to your senses… You should have redden their hineys a long time ago!"

"Haha!.. You're killing me, Aunt Jess," Lindsey erupted in laughter. "You sounded just like my mom."

"So what do you say?" Jessica asked her.

"Yes, of course. Our business is to redden bare bottoms and correct wayward behavior," Lindsey displayed a sarcastic smirk, "I know how feisty your daughter is. I actually had a run-in with her last year."

Lindsey went on, "She was over at my house, trying to act all cool, and swearing up a storm in front of my kids. Using the F-word and everything. I didn't threaten to spank her, I threatened to punch her lights out!"

"Oh, I had no idea," Jessica responded.

"It only lasted for a minute before she apologized immediately. She knew I meant business."

"So how should we do it?" Jessica asked, "I want to catch them off guard and take them by surprise. They'll know something is up if we tell them to come here to your office. I know you are coming over to my house tonight… Right?"

Lindsey paused for a moment to think. She then displayed a devilish grin on her pretty face.

"I have a great idea," she replied to Jessica, "Yes, I'm coming over to give Brittney and Katrina some of my old clothes. I'll be there with them as they pick, choose, and try on which items they want. Then, we'll arrange for my mom and Aunty Jeanine to come over to your house as well. She'll bring our implements and as soon as she gets there, we'll go to town on both of their rear-ends."

"That's perfect!" Jessica replied with a slight chuckle, "Melissa and Ryan will be going to their dad's house for the weekend, so it will just be us."

Jessica gave one last smile at Lindsey as she stood up from the chair, "I'll call your mom later to work out the payment and other details. I'll see you tonight, honey... And thank you!"

"No worries, Aunty Jess," Lindsey smirked, "They'll get what they deserve."

Chapter 23

The evening arrived and Lindsey was already over at her Aunt Jessica's home. She was enjoying spending time with her two younger cousins, Brittney and Katrina, and watching their eyes light up like children on Christmas morning as they fumbled through all of her old clothing.

"Oh My God!" Brittney squealed, "I love these jeans... I hope they fit!"

In record time, Brittney stripped down to her panties and slid into the form-fitting designer jeans that were once Lindsey's.

Katrina immediately smirked at her older cousin, "They fit you like a glove. Wait until your boyfriend sees the way your ass looks in them!"

"Here, try these, Kat," Lindsey chimed as she handed Katrina a pair of black exercise pants that had sexy cut-outs going down the legs.

Katrina wasted no time and pulled her jeans off and tossed them down on the living room floor. She stepped into the tight black leggings, did a slight upward jump to adjust them over her curvy hips, and glanced in the mirror.

"These are insane!" she commented to Lindsey. "What do you think?"

"You sure have the chubby Templeton ass. And so do you, Britt," Lindsey smirked, "I think just about anything you guys try on is going to look amazing on you."

"You should talk, basketball booty," Katrina laughed, "Your butt damn near poked our eyes out when you walked in the door!"

Lindsey proceeded to fumble through more of her clothes. This time, she pulled out a pair of faded ripped jeans for Katrina, and a super-cute sundress for Brittney.

"You guys can try these on next," she said excitedly as she handed them the clothing.

In the blink of an eye, Brittney and Katrina were back in their panties, as they removed the clothes they just had on. Once again, they put the new clothing on and smiled from ear to ear at the way it accented their amazing bodies.

"Oh My God! Oh My God!" Katrina jumped up and down, "These jeans ROCK!"

Just then, her mom, along with her twin sister Jeanine, and older sister Paula, entered the house.

"Hey mom! Hi Aunt Jeanine, Aunt Paula," Katrina smiled and continued checking herself out in the mirror.

Brittney followed with a similar hello to her two aunts, and then called out, "Mom, come check out this cute sundress cousin

Lindsey gave me!"

"That looks beautiful on you, Britt," Jeanine smiled as she walked into the living room to take a closer look at her daughter.

"I know right?" Brittney squealed and danced around from leg to leg.

Her little jig of a dance made Paula smirk, and immediately comment to Jeanine, "If you think she's dancing now, just wait, it's about to get even better."

Jeanine couldn't help but let out a little chuckle, knowing that it was only a matter of minutes before she would see her errant 25-year-old daughter, over the knee of her Aunt Paula, getting the comeuppance she deserved.

Lindsey continued to play it cool and handed the next set of outfits over to her cousins.

"Britt, try these jeans on. Kat, this skirt is going to look amazing on you," Lindsey announced, and then sent a cute smirk over to her Aunts Jessica and Jeanine, along with a now-is-the-time nod, to her mom.

Brittney and Katrina were so excited to try on these next pieces of clothing, that once again, at record speed, they stripped down to their panties. Just as they were about to try on these outfits, Aunt Paula abruptly interrupted them and made her move.

"I'll take these," she announced, and grabbed the clothes out of the hands of both her nieces.

"Girls, it's time we had a talk," she then forcefully grabbed their arms, and without hesitation, marched both of them across the room. "Move it!"

"Ouch!" Brittney yelped.

Katrina's feisty nature then reared it's head, "HEY! What the HELL? What are you..."

"Zip-it, Kat!" Lindsey quickly cut her off, and with furrowed eyebrows, she scolded, "Don't even think about saying another word! I don't want to hear a peep out of you!"

She latched onto Katrina's other arm and assisted her mom in putting her nieces in place with their backs pressed firmly against the living room wall.

"Girls, I'm absolutely appalled at everything that I've heard from both of your moms," Aunt Paula announced as she looked down at them, waiving her finger. "Your behavior, your attitude, your laziness, your disrespect… That does not fly in this family!"

Brittney and Katrina were totally caught off guard. They were still trying to process what was going on as they looked up at their Aunt Paula standing over them with fire in her eyes. Not only was she much taller than they were, Aunt Paula is a stature of a woman in every aspect of the word. Her size alone commanded attention from just about anyone that she met.

As kids, Brittney and Katrina always loved playing Wonder Woman with Aunt Paula, and sometimes, she even took on the role of an evil amazon monster coming to get them. Right now, the girls are having that same feeling as their 5 foot 10 inch Aunt has a look on her face like she's going to devour them.

Aunt Paula isn't just tall, she's also super-pretty and in tremendous shape for a 57-year-old woman. She was a stand-out basketball player in her school years, and even went on to play professionally. She's also no stranger to going to the gym and hardly ever misses an exercise class. Of course, her body has changed as she ages, but she isn't fat by any means. What she has are great genetics, including her family trademark, the over-sized, chubby "Templeton" butt.

The good thing is Aunt Paula has a nice amount of meat on her bones, which adds to her strength, even at her age. Along with that, she just looks intimidating with her mid-length blonde, slightly gray hair, and big hazel green eyes that right now were squinting so feverishly at her nieces, that it was making them shake with fear.

She released her grip on the arm of Brittney, but maintained her tight hold on Katrina's left bicep. She stared down at Katrina who was now literally shaking like a leaf. She scolded her with a tone so stern that it even sent shivers to everyone that was in the living room.

"Rumor has it that you're getting too big for your britches, young lady!" she scolded with a raised index finger, "Misbehaving, be disrespectful to your mom, not helping with the chores… Not to mention, your know-it-all-attitude and that filthy mouth of yours. I can assure you, all that non-sense is going to stop right here, right now!"

Katrina looked like a deer caught in the headlights of a speeding automobile as Aunt Paula stood over her. She knew better than to even say a word as Lindsey also stood by her side with that same fierce look on her face.

"And you!" Paula now released her grip on Katrina's arm, only to forcefully grab hold of Brittney's right bicep.

"I'm completely shocked at you, Brittney!" Aunt Paula scolded loudly, "Your mom tells me that your out drinking several nights a week, spending money like it's going out of style, and not pulling your weight with the housework."

Aunt Paula really escalated her voice now and made the scolding even more intense, "You are 25-years-old, young lady, and you're a nurse for God's sake. Your job is to care for people that are sick. You can't be out drinking until all hours of the morning and then expect to go to work and be 100%."

"That's absolutely ludicrous! I'm appalled at you… Both of YOU!"

Her voice was now so loud that it echoed off the living room walls.

"Oh yes, we are going to correct this behavior right now!" Aunt Paula sternly called out as she pulled a chair into the center of the room.

Chapter 24

Once Aunt Paula placed the chair exactly where she wanted it. She had it right in the center of the large living room, as she took her seat on it. She had such a stern and serious look on her face that just about anyone would be afraid to mess with her right now. She pointed to her sisters to take their place and stand next to their daughter's. She wanted them to get a full view of everything that was about to happen.

Aunt Paula then reached into her brown leather tote bag and took out several implements, including a wooden hairbrush, a good-sized Lexan paddle, another wooden paddle, and a thick leather strap. That look on her face and the scolding she just gave her nieces even had her sisters, Jeanine and Jessica, scared about what was going to happen to their daughter's rear-ends.

"Are you going to spank us, Aunt Paula?" Brittney asked with trepidation, already knowing the answer.

Aunt Paula now went on a rant and let out all the resentment and frustration that she'd been carrying for years.

"I'm going to do what both of your moms should have done a long time ago. They had been way too lenient with the two of you. I can't believe that neither of you have ever been spanked before. That's not the way it was for me growing up. Your grandmother, God rest her soul, never let me get away with anything."

Jessica had heard this so many times from her older sister that she couldn't help but chime in, "Oh come on, Paula. Don't bring up all this stuff again. Mom did the best she could. Everything changed when dad died. We all got spanked, not just you."

Paula got even more furious and was practically breathing fire now. She immediately retaliated back at her sister.

"HA! Are you kidding me, Jessica?"
"You and Jeanine hardly got spanked. Mom always took it easy on you guys. It was me that had to set the example because I was the oldest. She tanned my rear-end just about every week! And she didn't hold back!"

"You were not only the oldest," Jessica added, "You were also the smartest, the most athletic, and the most responsible. You were the only one in our family that received a full college scholarship. She had higher standards for you because you were in a league all of your own. You played professional basketball and made an insane amount of money. You're way more successful than both of us put together. Mom literally gloated when she talked about you."

Jeanine now jumped in and added, "That's the truth, Paula. Mom always referred to you as Paula Star… That was your nickname up until the day she passed away. She loved us all dearly, but you were her favorite, her star child… Jessica and I were always referred to as the twins. Hell, she couldn't even tell us apart. Half of the time she called me Jess."

Somehow, hearing that was exactly the validation that Paula needed after all these years. She wiped away a stray tear that fell from her eye and returned her focus back to the problems with her nieces.

"Fine!" Paula replied, still with a stern tone in her voice, "But that has nothing to do with how lenient you both have been with your kids. These girls should have had their plump bottoms reddened every time they misbehaved. Just ask Lindsey… I never let her get away with anything. And now, she's the same way with her own kids. Nothing works better at correcting bad behavior than a harsh spanking on a bare bottom."

"Bare bottom?" Katrina blurted out, "No way! You're not gonna pull our panties down!"

In the blink of an eye, Lindsey grabbed Katrina and forcefully spun her around. She pressed her face into the wall, raised her strong right arm up high, and delivered a slap so hard across Katrina's panties that it sounded like an explosion.

<SLAP>

"OOW!… Shit!" Katrina yelped in pain from the sting of her cousin's strong hand.

"ZIP IT!" Lindsey scolded, "There's more where that came from! I warned you… Not one word from you!"

She then spun Katrina back around to face her Aunt Paula, as she pressed the back of her shoulders into the wall again.

Aunt Paula now looked over at Brittney, "So to answer your question, Brittney. Not only am I going to spank you… but Lindsey is also going to spank you… both of you!"

"Here's how it's going to go." Aunt Paula continued with a thorough explanation.

"I'm going to redden your bottoms with my hand. Then Lindsey is going to do the same thing. After that, I'm going to give you both a dose of the hairbrush, and so is Lindsey. Then you will stand in the corner with your chubby bare bottoms on display until I give you permission to get dressed! Period! That's how it's going to go!"

That incredibly stern tone in Aunt Paula's voice was something that scared the daylights out of Brittney. She wisely kept her mouth shut, knowing that she was in for it.

"Turn around and face the wall! Rear-ends out!" Aunt Paula instructed.

Without hesitation, both Brittney and Katrina followed Aunt Paula's orders. They had their noses pressed into the wall of the living room with their cute and chubby rear-ends facing out.

"Nice panties, Katrina," Aunt Paula sarcastically called out. "They don't even come close to covering that plump melon of ass that you have!"

"They're not supposed to!" Katrina responded with an annoyed tone, "They're Brazilian style panties."

<SLAP>

Lindsey delivered another resounding hand slap over Katrina's underwear.

"Yeow!" Katrina squealed.

"NOT A WORD!" Lindsey yelled at her.

Aunt Paula couldn't help but chuckle at the sight of their super-cute, super-plump rear-ends that were peaking out of their panties. She stood up and took a closer look at each of them standing with their faces pressed into the wall wearing just their t-shirts and panties.

Aunt Paula reached down and squeezed Brittney's chubby cheeks, before giving them a few taps.

"What a melon," she smirked. "I'm going to enjoy spanking this bottom, Brittney Ann."

She then turned her attention to Katrina, who was in the same position. Now Aunt Paula's hands squeezed and closely inspected Katrina's over-sized booty.

"What a basketball," she commented with a sardonic tone, "Oh

Katrina Marie... I'm gonna have your rear-end bouncing up and down on my lap like it's a ball being dribbled my Micheal Jordan!"

After delivering her quirky humor, Aunt Paula returned to the chair and took her seat.

"Turn around and face me," she called out to them.

The girls didn't waste any time and quickly obeyed her command.

"Well, it's obvious," Aunt Paula chimed, "You girls sure inherited the famous Templeton rear-end. My God, your rear-ends are even bigger than mine and your mom's when we were your age. And that's saying a lot!"

Aunt Paula smirked then continued, "But as big as those rear-ends of yours are, they are also very beautiful. I won't speak for Lindsey, but I'm REALLY going to enjoy giving you both your first spanking."

Katrina was about to say something but luckily she caught herself before she engaged her mouth. Lindsey gave her a look, in addition to a raised hand, that instantly made her seal her lips.

Aunt Paula announced, "So... we can do this the easy way or we can do it the hard way."

She continued, "You can accept your punishment and take it like grown women. Otherwise, if you resist, kick, squirm, and backtalk either of us, it's going to be a lot worse for you... And trust me, I've seen Lindsey in action with some of the problem kids that we've disciplined in our company. You don't want to see her come undone!"

"I accept my punishment," Brittney quickly replied. "I know how strong cousin Lindsey is, I work out with her a lot."

Lindsey quickly took hold of Brittney's arm and walked her over to the chair that Aunt Paula was sitting in. Scared as can be, Brittney now stood on the right-hand side of her Aunt and was looking down at her thick legs that were showing themselves underneath her black business skirt. Brittney knew it would only be a few more seconds until she was draped across her Aunt's plushy lap.

"I want to say one other thing if I may," Brittney stated.

Aunt Paula looked up at her and nodded her head with a yes motion.

Brittney now had a few tears puddled in her eyes as she looked over at her mom, Jeanine.

"I'm really sorry, mom. I know I've been irresponsible, cranky, and just unable to deal with. I'll do better and this spanking may be just what I need to straighten up."

Aunt Paula now hiked her skirt up and high as she could and tapped her hands on her bare legs.

"Over my lap, Brittney Ann."

Brittney quickly maneuvered herself into position across her aunt's lap as her mom, her Aunt Jessica, Katrina, and Lindsey watched. Aunt Paula used her hands to further adjust Brittney into the exact position she wanted. Then, without any further ado, her large pretty hands slid inside the waist band of Brittney's panties and gave them a quick tug downward. Just like that, Brittney's rotund melon-shaped fanny was totally exposed. She was beyond embarrassed as her cute purple and pink striped cotton panties were now gathered around the middle of her chunky thighs.

"Look at those chubby cheeks!" Aunt Paula called out. "Like I said… I'm going to love sinking my hand into them!"

Needless to say, Brittney was not only incredibly embarrassed, but she also felt totally vulnerable being in this position.

Having her plump rear-end now completely exposed sent a chill down Brittney's spine as she remained in place over her Aunt Paula's lap. She braced herself waiting for the first slap to land and before she could take another breath, Aunt Paula delivered a slap so hard that it instantly made her scream.

<SLAP>

"OOW!"

Without pausing another second, Aunt Paula's large heavy right hand went to town on her niece's bare bottom.

<SLAP><SLAP><SLAP>
<SLAP><SLAP>

"YEOW!… Ow!… OOoo!" Brittney yelped like a little school girl as her buxom backside instantly changed color.

"MMMhmmm…" Aunt Paula scolded, "That's what I want to hear!… Let it out, Brittney Ann!"

Katrina, watching with her eyes opened as wide as possible, couldn't help but raise her eyebrows and cover her mouth with anxious fear.

<SLAP><SLAP>
<SLAP><SLAP><SLAP><SLAP>

Aunt Paula didn't hold back and now her slaps were precise as she made sure to evenly color both of Brittney's cantaloupe-sized cheeks.

"Ow!… I'm sorry, Aunt Paula… I'm sorry, mom," Brittney now squealed loudly, as the slaps really sunk in.

Her cute rear-end was now quivering on it's own, causing Aunt Paula to once again comment using her quirky humor.

"Look at that beautiful melon of a bottom shake!"

<SLAP><SLAP><SLAP>
<SLAP><SLAP>

"Ow!... Oooh!"

Aunt Paula scolded, "Keep those legs down, Missy!"

<SLAP><SLAP><SLAP><SLAP>

"OUCH!.. Yeow!" Brittney did her best to stay in place but she was still squirming all over her Aunt's well-sized lap.

Paula really laid into Brittney's bouncing butt as hard as she possibly could. She even scolded her with each slap.

"Don't...<SLAP> You... <SLAP> Ever... <SLAP><SLAP> Misbehave... <SLAP> or Disrespect...<SLAP> Your Mom Again, Brittany Ann!"

<SLAP><SLAP><SLAP>

Brittney now graduated into a steady, slightly out of breath, sobbing, "OOW!... Oh God!"

"God isn't going to help this plump derriere of yours now, my dear," Aunt Paula commented. "It's all mine and I'm going to give it just what it deserves!"

"Lindsey, hand me my hairbrush, please," Aunt Paula announced.

"No!!! No!" Brittney pleaded, "I'm sorry, Aunt Paula."

She took the hairbrush from her daughter, clenched her jaw tightly, squinted her pretty eyes, and delivered a flurry of spanks with zero mercy.

<SMACK><CRACK><CRACK><SMACK>
<WHACK><CRACK>

"OOOOW… Noooo!"

Brittney was now flapping all over her Aunt's lap and crying her eyes out. Her once pale white chubby cheeks were now totally discolored.

There were no other words for it, Aunt Paula's hairbrush spanking was harsh and unforgiving. After that series of spanks, she took a moment to stare down at Brittney's bottom. She smirked at the sight of her well-marked cheeks in various shades of red. Aunt Paula even squeezed them several times to further embarrass her defiant niece.

"Look at this bright red tooshie!" she called out to everyone in the room watching. "It looks like a volleyball crossed with an apple!"

Aunt Paula's joke made her daughter Lindsey laugh out loud, which further added to Brittney's shame. Paula smirked at her daughter and commented.

"I bet you can't wait to get your hands on your cousin's fanny."

Lindsey smirked back at her mom, "She's really in for it when I get my hands on her… Both of them are!"

The super-harsh tone of Lindsey's voice really sent shivers up and down Brittney's spine. Her fanny was already on fire and completely covered with the bright red marks of her Aunt Paula's large handprints, as well as the hairbrush. As for Katrina, she was trying her best to appear all cool, but deep down inside she had the nervousness of a thousand butterflies flapping around in her stomach.

"It's her turn," Paula called out to Lindsey, as she stared over at Katrina.

Lindsey pulled Brittney off her mom's lap and led her back into place against the wall.

"Keep those undies down," Lindsey instructed Brittney, who was now standing with her vagina completely exposed.

Just as Brittney attempted to move her hands over her vagina, Lindsey quickly interrupted with a super-hard slap.

<SLAP>

"OOOW!"

Lindsey's intense slap landed on the front of Brittney's meaty left thigh and instantly made her dance in place.

"And keep those arms at your sides!" Lindsey scolded her.

Then, with an assertive and stern look on her face, Lindsey approached Katrina.

"Your turn, Princess!" she stated with a cocky attitude. "I really can't wait to spank your ass!"

"She's all mine first," Aunt Paula called out. "Bring her over here."

Chapter 25

Lindsey gave a quick nod to her mom as she reached out and took hold of Katrina's arm.

"Lets go!… Move it!"

Katrina now found herself standing on the right-hand side of her amazon-sized Aunt Paula.

"Do you have anything to say, Katrina Marie?" Aunt Paula asked.

"Yeah, I do," Katrina replied back in that cocky attitude of hers, "I can't believe you guys have planned this. All of you… Aunt Jeanine, you, cousin Lindsey, and worse of all you, mom!"

"You and Brittney left us no choice," Jessica replied back to her daughter. "You need to get your act together. Us moms are tired, we work hard, and organize our households. The last thing we want to do is deal with attitudes like yours."

"This is done out of love," Aunt Paula added. "Over my knee!"

Lindsey kept her grip on Katrina as she pulled her in place over Aunt Paula's lap. She took it a step further and didn't even wait for her mom to pull Katrina's panties down. Instead, Lindsey walked behind Katrina, and with one aggressive tug, yanked her panties completely off her legs.

"Thank you, Lindsey," her mom smirked as she looked down at

Katrina's more than ample bare bottom.

"Oh, My, my, my," Aunt Paula chuckled as she squeezed Katrina's plump fluffy ass cheeks, "I'm going to enjoy making these cheeks jiggle."

"Not as much as I am!" Lindsey commented. "She's had it coming to her since last year when she acted out around my kids. Swearing up a storm, and acting all entitled!"

"Is that so?" Aunt Paula's eyes glared down at Katrina's ass with full intensity.

She then raised her hand high in the air and delivered the first slap.

<SLAP>

It landed on the lower right side of Katrina's bubble butt, right above her upper thigh. To everyone's surprise, Katrina didn't make much of a sound.

"Ah! She's trying to hold it in," Aunt Paula called out in an annoyed tone. "Let's see how long that will last!"

<SLAP><SLAP><SLAP><SLAP>

"OOO!... Ouch!"

And just like that, Katrina's silence came to an end as she flat-out screamed from the sting of her Aunt Paula's heavy hand. Stern Aunty Paula went right into scolding in a super loud voice with every slap she administered.

<SLAP> YOU… <SLAP> BETTER…<SLAP> STRAIGHTEN… <SLAP> UP…<SLAP> AND STOP… <SLAP> ACTING LIKE A… <SLAP> SPOILED BRAT!

<SLAP><SLAP><SLAP>
<SLAP><SLAP>

"OOOW!… I'm sorry!" Katrina yelped as her ass jiggled uncontrollably after each slap.

<SLAP><SLAP><SLAP><SLAP>

"DO YOU HEAR ME, KATRINA MARIE?" Aunt Paula scolded her about as loud as her voice could go.

"YES!… OUCH!" Katrina was now bouncing like a ball in the street all over her aunt's soft well-cushioned lap.

Once again, Paula signaled for the hairbrush, as Lindsey handed it over to her with a smile.

Katrina saw this and immediately went into an all-out plea, "No!… Please... I'm sorry, I'm sorry!"

Her plea was useless and fell on deaf ears as her Aunt Paula raised the brush high and delivered it with precision.

<CRACK><CRACK><SMACK>
<SMACK><CRACK><CRACK><SMACK>

"WHAAA!… OUCH!" Katrina was now bawling her eyes out.

Her overly plump bottom quickly displayed the welts from the brush as it changed color before everyone's eyes. It was such a deep red that it looked like a giant candy apple. Aunt Paula now extended several hard swats with the brush across the back of her chunky upper thighs.

<SMACK><CRACK><SMACK>

"UUUH!… OOOO!" Katrina's eyes continued to flow like a faucet as the tears ran down her face.

"Save some of that fanny for me, mom," Lindsey called out to her mom.

Aunt Paula smirked as she looked down and admired her work on Katrina's thoroughly bruised bubble-butt.

"Get up, young Lady!" Aunt Paula ordered.

The minute Katrina's feet touched the ground she began to feverishly rub her tender cheeks and hop around. She went into this cute little dance that had her hopping in place, while at the same time, rubbing her jiggly bottom.

Lindsey couldn't help but smirk at her younger cousin finally getting the harsh discipline she deserved. She quickly grabbed her by the arm and marched her in place right back to where she was standing next to Brittney.

Aunt Paula now stood up and walked over them. Brittany and Katrina, completely exposed from the waist down, stood with their arms at their sides. To the left of them, stood their mom's Jeanine and Jessica, with a more than satisfied look on their faces.

"Let this be a lesson to both of you," Aunt Paula scolded once again, as she towered over them. "If I ever get a report from either of my sisters that you misbehaved, I can assure you, that strap is going to come out and it will be far worse!"

She glared into their teary eyes, "Is that understood?"

"Yes, Ma'am... Yes, Aunt Paula," quickly emerged from their mouths.

"I'm sorry, Ma'am. I've definitely learned my lesson," Brittney quickly apologized. "Please don't let cousin Lindsey spank us."

Brittney knew that as hard as Aunt Paula just spanked her, that a spanking from Lindsey would be even worse. She worked out with her older cousin on a regular basis, so she was well aware of just how strong Lindsey really was.

"Oh, she's going to spank you alright!" Aunt Paula quickly replied.

Once again, her plea was useless and fell on deaf ears as Aunt Paula followed up with, "You can be sure of that!"

Brittney and Katrina followed every move of their stern warrior-sized Aunt Paula as she slowly walked away with purpose to talk to her daughter. They watched intently as she whispered into Lindsey's ear. They were trembling like two little school girls caught in a snowstorm as they watched their sexy, super-athletic older cousin walk over to them. As stunningly beautiful as Lindsey is, right now she had that get-down-to-business look on her face, which made her appear downright scary.

Lindsey then positioned herself right next to her Aunt Jessica as she starred intently at her young cousins.

"If you think my mom's spanking was hard... Wait until I get a hold of you!" Lindsey sternly warned them. "Especially you, Katrina! Your behind is mine!"

It was obvious that Lindsey really had it in for Katrina. Regardless of that, they both knew it would be just a matter of seconds before she grabbed one of them and blistered their bottoms. Brittney and Katrina now looked at each other and silently wondered who was going to be the first chosen by Lindsey.

Their question was quickly answered as they opened their eyes as wide as saucers when their strong cousin reached out and made her move.

Chapter 26

"OUCH!"

A loud yelp quickly filled the room as Lindsey applied a vice-like grip.

"MOVE IT!" She scolded and started marching back toward her mom, who was already waiting with the hairbrush in her hand.

"Are you serious?"

"We are more than serious," Paula called out as she looked into the eyes of her totally surprised sister Jessica.

"You are NOT going to SPANK me!" Jessica defiantly emphasized.

"What's the matter, mom?" Katrina quickly chimed, "Afraid to get your big butt spanked?"

Lindsey quickly replied in her stern voice, "Just like my mom said to your daughters, Aunt Jess… We can do this the easy way or we can do this the hard way!"

"Remove your skirt, Jessica," Paula instructed her.

"I'm about to make up for some of the spankings that mom never gave you," she warned her sister.

"This is crazy!" Jeanine chimed in from across the room.

"I suggest you keep quiet because you're next," Paula warned Jeanine, with a raised finger.

"Take it like a woman," Paula called out to Jessica. "Now remove that skirt!"

"Fine!" Jessica stomped her leg, "I'll take your spanking."

Jessica kicked her high heels off, and unfastened her black skirt. She then slid it down her legs and stepped out of it. Her amazingly plump but absolutely round and beautiful ass was easily peaking out of the side of her black-laced panties.

"Over my knee, cupcake!" Paula razzed her sister.

The very second Jessica maneuvered herself over Paula's lap, she felt her older sister's hands tug her panties all the way down to her ankles.

"Now this is for sure a TEMPLETON ass!" Paula smirked as her eyes took in the size and shape of her younger sister's bare bottom.

Out of everyone in the family, Jessica's butt was the biggest and most plump. However, as big and as plump as it was, it was also beautifully round and very sexy. Even though Paula also had the famous Templeton family's chubby type of ass, she was a bit envious of her twin sisters bodies. They were nowhere near as tall as her, and had always look good no matter what outfit they wore.

Paula then remembered how just about every boy in school wanted to get at Jessica's ass. She often had to blacken the eyes of many of them for gawking and making lewd remarks to both of her younger siblings, especially Jessica.

The wait was now over and the years of being frustrated finally came to an end. Paula scowled down at her sister's innocent chubby white cheeks and delivered a barrage of hand slaps all across Jessica's rear-end.

<SLAP><SLAP><SLAP>
<SLAP><SLAP><SLAP>
<SLAP>

Jessica immediately let her pain be known as she yelped from the sting of her older sister's heavy hand.

"OOO!… Yeoow!"

"That's it!" Paula smirked, "It's about time this chubby fanny of yours got what it deserved!"

<SLAP><SLAP>

"OUCH!" Jessica squealed.

She even started kicking her chubby legs upward in a natural reaction to the pain happening all over her cheeks.

"Keep those legs down!" Paula scolded her.

Lindsey reacted and quickly moved in. She took a kneeling down position, and actually grabbed hold of her Aunt Jessica's legs. Paula's slaps continued to fly hard and precise all over her Jessica's ample behind.

<SLAP><SLAP><SLAP>

"OOOOW!... Ouch!"

Jessica's mobility was greatly taken away by her powerful niece holding down her legs. All that she could do was wiggle and squirm across Paula's lap, and that she did... feverishly.

"Look at this hiney JIGGLE!" Paula smirked as she watched Jessica's rear-end jiggle like a bowl of Jello.

She then signaled for Lindsey to pass her the hairbrush, and within two seconds, Jessica's yelps turned into a full-on howl.

<CRACK><SMACK><CRACK><CRACK>
<SMACK>

"OOOW! No, Paula!... Ouch!" Jessica actually had tears flowing from her eyes as her ass was thoroughly welted.

Paula gave one last flurry with the hairbrush, before passing it back to Lindsey.

"Here!" she told her daughter, "Your turn. Show your Aunt Jessica just how hard you spank!"

Paula literally yanked Jessica to her feet as Lindsey took her seat on the chair. She then pulled her aunt onto her muscular legs and adjusted her into the perfect position across her lap. Lindsey pulled the panties off that were gathered around her aunt's ankles and tossed them on the floor.

She handed the hairbrush back to her mom, and commented, "Mom, hold this for a second. I want to spank Aunt Jess's chubby ass with my hand first."

As Lindsey raised her right arm up high, Brittany and Katrina couldn't help but notice the insane muscle tone of their older cousin's physique. They knew a spanking from her was going to be even worse than from Aunt Paula… And boy, were they right!

Lindsey delivered a rapid fire series of spanks so hard to her Aunt Jessica's jiggly ass that it sounded like an army of machine guns firing off in the living room.

<SLAP><SLAP><SLAP>
<SLAP><SLAP>
<SLAP><SLAP>
<SLAP>

"OOOUCH!" Jessica was howling louder than ever and went right back to frantically kicking her legs.

Of course, this didn't fly with Lindsey, who was more than used to handling naughty teenagers that did this. She quickly placed her muscular right leg over Jessica's and then forcefully clamped down like a scissors. She delivered several more slaps with the utmost force to her Aunt's quivering cheeks.

<SLAP><SLAP><SLAP><SLAP>

Jessica now tried to reach back with her right hand to cover her buxom booty and block the slaps. Of course, Lindsey quickly ended that by pinning it to her lower back. She then looked up at her mom and called for the hairbrush.

"Let this be a lesson for you as well, Aunt Jessica," Lindsey scolded. "Don't ever let Katrina treat you with any disrespect again!"

Lindsey raised that wooden brush high and administered a series of spanks that had her Aunt Jessica squealing.

<CRACK><SMACK><CRACK>
<CRACK><SMACK>

"OOW!... OKAY! OUCH!" Jessica pleaded as Lindsey continued to really blister her bottom.

<SMACK><SMACK><CRACK>

Jessica now clenched her ass cheeks as tight as she could in a natural reaction. Squeezing her rear-end this tight made some of Jessica's natural dimples and cellulite appear. This made Lindsey smile and comment as she focused on her Aunt's plump bottom.

"Look at her clenching those chubby cheeks," Lindsey smirked, "You can tighten all you want, Aunt Jess… I'm used to seeing bare bottom clench like that… I can promise you, it's not going to help!"

And with that, Lindsey delivered her final flurry with the hairbrush.

<CRACK><SMACK><SMACK><SMACK> <SMACK><CRACK>

To say that she gave her older Aunt Jess a spanking would be an understatement. Lindsey really blistered her super-plump backside. She then pulled her Aunt Jessica off her lap, and just like Katrina, once Jessica's legs touched the floor, she went into an all-out dance. Her totally bruised fanny jiggled uncontrollably as she bounced up and down rubbing her bare bottom.

Paula couldn't help but smile in delight as she now started marching Jeanine by the arm into the center of the floor. She then quickly traded places with Lindsey, and sat down on the chair.

"Your turn, Jeanine!" she called out.

Chapter 27

"Pants down, Jeanine," Paula instructed her younger sister as she looked up at her.

Jeanine didn't waste any time as she knew it would only be worse for her. She quickly pulled her black and white hound-tooth patterned pants down to her knees. She then placed herself willingly over Paula's lap and within two seconds, just like everyone else, her panties were tugged down, and she was yelping in pain.

Paula proceeded to discipline Jeanine in the same way that she did Jessica. She made sure there wasn't an inch of white skin remaining on her fluffy ass cheeks. To everyone's surprise, Jeanine actually took the hand spanking much better than her sister Jessica. For the most part, she managed to stay in place and totally refrained from kicking her legs upward.

Of course, this all changed once Paula picked up the hairbrush and really started adding the red welts to her pumpkin-shaped ass. At this point, her daughter Lindsey quickly assisted by now holding her Aunt Jeanine's legs down as her mom profusely administered the hairbrush.

In similar fashion to the others, once she pulled Jeanine off her lap and back onto her feet, another spanking dance was seen by all. Jeanine immediately began rubbing her plump reddened bottom as she hopped, then squatted down in place.

Lindsey didn't even let her Aunt Jeanine get her bearings as she quickly grabbed her by the arm and tugged her right back over her lap. Her big beautiful emerald green eyes now looked down on her aunt's ample rear-end as she raised her right hand high over her head. Once again, the sound of loud slaps coupled with yelps and pleas filled the living room.

<SLAP><SLAP><SLAP>
<SLAP><SLAP>
<SLAP><SLAP><SLAP>

"Ooouch!… OOOww!" Aunt Jeanine squealed at the force of her niece's hand spanking.

It only got worse for her when, after another round of relentless slaps, Lindsey picked up the hairbrush. Her young niece proceeded to deliver such an intense flurry that it made her Aunt Jeanine's mascara run down her face from the amount of tears that fell from her eyes.

When the spanking was over, Lindsey marched her Aunt Jeanine back in place, standing against the wall. Of course, Jeanine waddled like a penguin since her pants were still gathered around her ankles. Lindsey smirked as she then stepped back and stood next to her mom.

"Step out of your pants, Aunt Jeanine," Lindsey instructed her.

Jeanine quickly obeyed, and like the others, she was now totally naked from the waist down.

Lindsey, along with her mom, Paula, continued to embarrass them as they stared intensely at each one of them. They went down the line, from left to right, and first looked at their faces before casting stares at their naked bodies.

They first looked at Jeanine standing there, with tears still in her eyes, and her vagina in full sight. Jessica was next to her with her arms at her side, followed by the two younger girls, Brittney and Katrina.

"Let this be a lesson that none of you should ever forget," Paula scolded.

She then directed her words at her two younger twin sisters.

"I hope both of you start spanking your kids if they ever disrespect you again. And if you need help, you can call Lindsey or me!"

Jessica and Jeanine acknowledged, as they both gave Paula a nod of their heads.

"Now turn around… Fannies out!" Paula instructed.

Like a synchronized dance team, they all spun around, hovered in the corner, with their faces to the wall. Paula and Lindsey now took in the full view of the four totally red and bruised bottoms all in line, one after the other.

"Look at these four plump basketball bottoms," Aunt Paula commented, as she went down the line and squeezed each one.

"15 minutes... Hands on your heads," She ordered and set an alarm on her cell phone.

The level of embarrassment for each of them to be standing there naked from the waist down was almost as bad as the spanking. The fifteen minutes felt like several hours, especially for Brittney and Katrina. Up to this point, they had been spanked by Aunt Paula, but not by their cousin Lindsey. They couldn't help but silently wonder if cousin Lindsey had forgotten and was going to let them slide. The time finally elapsed and the alarm sounded.

"Turn around, hands at your sides," Paula instructed them.

Once again, each of the ladies felt utterly embarrassed about being exposed and having their vagina in full view. Brittney and Katrina's eyes were now completely focused on their cousin Lindsey, who was whispering in the ear of her mom.

Paula, in turn, whispered back in Lindsey's ear. After a few more of these secret conversations, Paula's head nodded in agreement as they pulled away from each other.

Aunt Paula then made an announcement, "Jeanine and Jessica, you two can get dressed and come stand over here by me."

The twin sisters followed their older sister's orders and within a few minutes they were now standing next to Paula and Lindsey.

This left Brittany and Katrina extremely vulnerable as they stood against the wall facing everyone.

"Why can't we get dressed?" Katrina shot back at her Aunt Paula with a slight attitude.

"Haha!" Aunt Paula chuckled, "Because Lindsey still has yet to get at your rear-ends, and I can't wait to watch my daughter handle both of you."

Brittney's head titled downward and Katrina's face literally dropped several inches with a frown so big it was the size of a rainbow.

"First things first," Lindsey called out.

"We can continue trying on my old clothing tomorrow, after my yard sale. I expect both of you to be at my house by 9am... And be prepared to work... On Sunday, you both are going to do whatever chores your mom's lay out for you. This means laundry, vacuuming, dusting, cooking, grocery shopping, etc. Is that understood?"

Both girls acknowledged their older cousin with a quick nod of their heads.

"In addition, you are both grounded. Aside from going to your jobs, you are not to go out or get together with your friends for 1 week. If I find out that either of you do not follow these orders, I will get at your cheeks again and give double of what you got today. Then, I will make you both stand against this wall again, and this time, I will make sure that Ryan, Melissa, and my three kids get to see your big red bottoms!"

"Is that clear?"

Again, both girls remained silent but gave Lindsey a nod of their heads.

"Katrina, go stand next to your mom," Lindsey ordered. "I saving your cheeks for last!"

Chapter 28

Katrina immediately walked over and took her position next to her mom. She stood there with her eyes glued to her cousin Lindsey as she watched her approach Brittney.

There Brittany was, still trembling as she stood with her back pressed against the living room wall. She already had tears puddled in her eyes as Lindsey slowly approached her.

Lindsey, took the time to roll up her shirt sleeves with each step she took toward her younger cousin. At 5 foot 9, Lindsey was already 4 to 5 inches taller than Brittney. However, right now with her high heels on and Brittney standing there in her bare feet, totally exposed from the waist down, she really towered over her.

Brittney, at 25, couldn't help but feel like a naughty child as she looked up and watched Lindsey coming closer to her with that stern look on her pretty face.

"I'm really sorry, Lindsey," she quickly sobbed, hoping to curb some of the punishment.

"You know how much I love you, Cous," Lindsey replied, "But this spanking is something that you really need. I've been telling you for months that you've been out partying way too much. Haven't I?"

"You have, Linds," Brittney replied back. "I should've listened to you."

"You're 25 years-old, with full-on responsibilities. You are not some wayward child!" Lindsey scolded her. "Since you want to act like a naughty child, I'm going to spank you like I do my own kids... Only ten times harder!"

Lindsey forcefully grabbed hold of Brittney's left arm, spun her around, and as she remained standing, she unleashed a series of slaps. The force of these slaps were so hard across Brittney's cute chubby ass, that she squealed like a banshee and immediately began dancing from leg to leg.

<SLAP><SLAP><SLAP><SLAP>
<SLAP><SLAP><SLAP>

"OOOW!.. I'm sorry!.... I'm sorry, Linds! OUCH!"

Lindsey's hand slaps were beyond relentless as she continued to put all of her body weight into each swing.

<SLAP><SLAP>
<SLAP><SLAP><SLAP>
<SLAP><SLAP>

"Oh My GOD!.... OOW!... I'm SORRY!" Brittney cried out.

"Damn right you're sorry!" Lindsey scolded as she delivered slap after slap.

"I will redden this plump bottom of yours in a heartbeat if you don't straighten up!"

<SLAP>
<SLAP><SLAP>

"Got it?" Lindsey continued to scold her as she extended some hard slaps down the back of her upper thighs.

"Ooow!… Yes! Aaah!... I got it!... OUCH!" Brittney loudly wailed as the tears flowed down her face.

This hand spanking that her strong, physically fit, cousin was giving her was even harder than the hairbrush spanking that Brittney had just received from her Aunt Paula. Lindsey knew exactly how to deliver the most severe hand spanking that she could. She continued to hold onto Brittney's left bicep and put all her body weight into every slap. Being a cross-fit champion and knowing how to use leverage, Lindsey drew the extra force from her curvy hips and engaged them into every swing, just like a professional tennis player.

<SLAP><SLAP><SLAP>
<SLAP><SLAP>

She delivered one last flurry, that had her younger cousin crying a river, before she paused and pulled the chair over to her.

"Bend over the back of that chair!… And stick your fanny out as far as possible!" Lindsey ordered as she picked up the clear acrylic Lexan paddle.

Brittney was now bent over the back of the wooden chair with her bruised red rump arched out as far as possible.

"Count! And tell your mom that you are sorry!" Lindsey sternly stated as she tapped the paddle several times lightly on Brittney's bottom.

After scoping out the exact area of Brittney's cheeks that she planned to color with the paddle, Lindsey pulled it back and swung.

<WHACK>

"OOO!... 1... I'm sorry, mom!" Brittney yelped and again bounced up and down.

"Get back over that chair!" Lindsey quickly pushed her back into position.

<WHACK>

"YEOWCH!... 2... I'm sorry, mom!"

"Arch that butt out," Lindsey ordered her.

The very moment Brittney arched her bare bottom outward, Lindsey delivered another merciless swat.

<WHACK>

"OOOw!... Oh My GOD!... OUCH!... 3... I'm s-o-r-r-y, m-o-m!"

Her apologies were now almost unrecognizable as she sobbed like a child.

"One more," Lindsey stated, "Rear-end out!"

Brittney squealed and positioned herself in place for the last one. Lindsey carefully planned and tapped the paddle several times on her cheeks before pulling it back and swinging hard.

<WHACK>

"OOOW!" Brittney immediately squatted down in place as her chubby butt jiggled uncontrollably.

"Did you forget something?" Lindsey called out.

"4... I'm... s-o-r-r-y... M-o-m..." she could barely get the words out from sobbing so much.

Lindsey took her by the arm and led her next to the others. Brittney immediately hugged her mom and repeated her apology, before she vigorously started rubbing her butt in an attempt to soothe the pain.

"Now speaking of acting like a naughty child..." Lindsey smirked as she turned her attention to Katrina standing against the wall.

"Hold this, Aunt Jess," she handed the paddle to Katrina's mom.

Lindsey now took hold of Katrina's arm and marched her to the corner of the living room. Once there, she spun her around so that she was facing her. Even though Katrina was scared as hell, she did her best not to show her fear. She displayed this totally annoyed, even cocky smirk on her face that really got on Lindsey's last nerve.

Chapter 29

"You better wipe that smirk off your face, Katrina!" Lindsey scolded her.

"I can't believe your gonna let her spank me, mom," Katrina now lashed out. "This is fucking bullshit!"

"Whoa!" Aunt Paula replied loudly, after hearing those swears come out of Katrina's mouth.

"Knock it off, Katrina," her mom now chimed in. "This is exactly what you need!"

"Really Lindsey?" Katrina now directed her anger at her older cousin.

"Let me guess… Now is the part where you tell me how much you love me before you tan my ass… Right?" she sarcastically stated.

"You know how close I am to you and Britt. I love you guys like sisters," Lindsey clearly stated, "But what's right is right. You are acting like an entitled, self-serving, irresponsible brat!"

"Oh, excuse me!" Katrina blasted back with even more attitude. "And you never acted like this when you were my age?"

"Ha! I was exactly like you, Katrina," Lindsey quickly responded, "So I know first hand what it took to straighten me out. My mom didn't stand for it and she never hesitated to strap my ass everytime I acted up. I wouldn't be able to sit comfortably for days!"

"I sure did!" Aunt Paula chimed in.

"You need to chill-out, Kat," Brittney called out from across the room, "Loose the attitude… You're making it worse for yourself."

"How much worse could it be?" Katrina continued mouthing off, "Lindsey gonna beat my ass either way. It's FUCKING ridiculous!"

"That's it!... I had enough of this mouth!" Lindsey was now fuming with fire coming out of her veins.

She aggressively pinned Katrina against the wall, then reached down, and literally pulled her t-shirt over her head. Once she got the shirt off her body, she hastily tossed it on the floor. Now only one item of clothing remained on Katrina's cute body and that was her bra. In a matter of seconds, that was addressed as Lindsey grabbed onto her arm, spun her around so that her ass was facing out, and pressed her entire body forcefully into Katrina's.

"You want to act like a naughty child… Fine!… I'll strip you down to your birthday suite just like I do my own kids when they misbehave!" Lindsey scolded in a loud stern voice.

Lindsey had Katrina pinned so hard into the corner that her nose was now pressed against the wall. Using all her strength, she continued to hold Katrina in place as she quickly unsnapped her bra, and yanked it off her.

Katrina was now totally naked and really felt the embarrassment as Lindsey unleashed a series of the hardest slaps that she ever gave anyone in her entire life!

<SLAP><SLAP><SLAP>
<SLAP><SLAP>

"OOOW!… Ooh!" Katrina's super-fluffy ass cheeks were now bouncing and jiggling all over the place like gelatin on a plate.

Lindsey kept her intense focus, and used her strength to keep her younger cousin held tightly in place. She swung her muscular right arm as hard as she possibly could and also used the strength of her hips to step into every single slap she delivered.

<SLAP><SLAP><SLAP><SLAP>

"OOW!.. OKAY... OKAY! I'm Sorry!" Katrina bawled her eyes out.

Lindsey continued to hold her in a standing position, slightly against the wall, as she administered a number of unrelenting hand slaps to her hiney.

<SLAP><SLAP><SLAP>
<SLAP><SLAP>

"WHAAA!… OOOUCH!… I'm Sorry!" Katrina bawled.

Not only were the tears now falling like rain from Katrina's pretty eyes, but she was also dancing around like her feet were on hot coals. Lindsey quickly moved in and secured her over her curvy hip, then proceeded to deliver another relentless flurry of hand slaps.

<SLAP><SLAP>
<SLAP><SLAP><SLAP>
<SLAP>

"OUCH!… Lindsey, I'm sorry!" Katrina pleaded.

Being the no-nonsense disciplinarian that she was, Lindsey then grabbed hold of Katrina's right ear lobe with a forceful pinch, and literally pulled her towards the kitchen.

"Let's go! Move it, Missy!" Lindsey commanded.

Katrina did all she could to keep up as she was being forcefully yanked by her earlobe. The pain she was feeling on her bare bottom, coupled with the way her older cousin was aggressively handling and disciplining her, made her forget all about being completely naked from head to toe. Right now it didn't matter that her perky boobs, her young, well-groomed vagina, and her beyond bouncing booty were being seen by everyone. All she could think about was moving in the direction that Lindsey was pulling her in.

Lindsey assertively maneuvered Katrina so that she was bent over the kitchen sink. She positioned herself directly behind her and pressed her entire body into Katrina's to hold her in place. Lindsey then grabbed a bar of soap, quickly wet it under the faucet, and vigorously rubbed it between her hands. Once the soap created enough lather, she gave a quick tug on Katrina's long blonde hair, forcing her young cousin to open her mouth.

"Ooow!" Katrina yelped.

"STICK OUT THAT TONGUE!" Lindsey scolded in an elevated voice.

Once Katrina did, Lindsey wasted no time and proceeded to scrub her entire tongue with that bar of Ivory soap. In a matter of seconds, Katrina was spitting, coughing out soap bubbles, and at the same time, crying her eyes out. None of that mattered to Lindsey. She didn't let up one bit and proceeded to thoroughly wash every inch of Katrina's mouth out like she was a naughty child.

Being a super-stern, spanking mom with three kids of her own, Lindsey was no stranger to doing this. Plus, she and her mom often used this type of punishment, along with a spanking, when they disciplined wayward boys and girls at their office. In fact, Lindsey herself did it so much that Paula always joked about how she should buy stock in the company that makes the brand of soap she uses.

"Keep that mouth open, young lady!" she further scolded Katrina as she vigorously rubbed the soap all over her tongue.

Lindsey made sure she shoved her fingers and that bar of soap all around the inside of Katrina's mouth. She then instructed her, with a stern voice.

"Bite it! Hold that bar in your mouth, Katrina!"

As Katrina clamped down on the bar of soap, Lindsey went into the other room and grabbed her favorite implement, a thick leather strap. This was the one she reached for often to use on very naughty boys and girls. This wasn't just an ordinary leather belt. This was an actual Canadian prison strap that measured about 24 inches long and 3 inches wide. It had a comfortable, very secure handle that was accented by a rope that went around the wrist.

Katrina remained in place, weeping her eyes out, bent over the kitchen sink, not even thinking about what was next. She was crying so hard that she didn't even realize that Lindsey had slipped away and now had the thick strap clenched tightly in her right hand.

That soon ended as Lindsey introduced the strap to Katrina's bare bottom. She swung so hard and with such a vengeance, that it sounded like an explosion went off when it connected to Katrina's hiney.

<CRACK>

Katrina's howls were greatly muffled from holding the bar of soap in her mouth. Lindsey went on and delivered three more of the hardest, most relentless swats imaginable with that strap. It was for sure the hardest strapping that Lindsey had ever administered to anyone.

<CRACK><WHACK><CRACK>

The sound of that strap hitting Katrina's bare ass consecutively, sounded like a new world war had just begun in the Templeton's kitchen.

"Keep that fanny out, Katrina!" Lindsey scolded. "And that bar better stay in your mouth!"

Katrina's cries continued to be muffled as she bit down harder on the bar of soap. Lindsey delivered one final flurry of 4 swats in a matter of seconds that made Katrina literally jump up and down in a frantic way.

<WHACK><CRACK><CRACK><SMACK>

Lindsey, finally satisfied that Katrina received the discipline she needed, removed the bar of soap from her mouth and marched her right back into the corner of the living room.

"20 minutes!" She called out. "Keep that rear-end of yours out, and don't even think about rubbing it!"

Katrina was now sobbing uncontrollably in the corner of the living room. Her chubby ass was quivering and shaking involuntarily. It had a number of deep red stripes going across it, that made it look like the flag of the United States.

"Go stand next to your cousin," Lindsey now ordered Brittany.

Within seconds, Brittany took her position next to Katrina, with her puffy, well marked rear-end facing outward.

"Remove your shirt, Brittney Ann," Lindsey now commanded, "Your bra as well!"

Brittney quickly followed her orders, and in the blink of an eye, she was also completely naked. Lindsey took a few steps backwards and stood in line with her mom and her two aunts. Now all of them took in the sight of Brittney's and Katrina's thoroughly bruised, thoroughly swollen bare bottoms.

"Does this satisfy your requirements?" Lindsey asked her two aunts.

"Yes, dear!" Aunt Jeanine quickly replied.

"Absolutely!" Aunt Jessica chimed in. "And I won't hesitate to hire you again if I need to."

At that moment, the twin sisters felt this spanking would not only be something their daughters would remember for the rest of their lives, but it would also be the catalyst for better behavior. They also felt their older sister Paula would finally release some of the resentment she'd been carrying most of her life.

"Arms on your head… Turn around and face us," Lindsey instructed Brittany and Katrina.

The young cousins wasted no time in following her orders as they now stood facing them in their birthday suits.

"Do you have anything to say?" Lindsey asked them.

"Again, I want to apologize to my mom… I'm really sorry, and I'll do better," Brittany quickly replied.

"M-e… t-o-o," Katrina added, still sobbing. "I'm really s-o-r-r-y, m-o-m."

Katrina could barely get those words out as she went right back to crying.

"Turn back around, rear-ends out… 20 minutes!" Lindsey once again commanded.

Just then, Paula's cell phone rang. The custom ring tone indicated that it was a call from the office.

She answered, "Crimson Bottoms Discipline Services. This is Paula."

Paula went on to have a conversation with her customer.

"Oh yes, hello Ms. Evans… How are you?… Oh My… Really?… Your two boys were responsible for that?… No, you're totally right, this calls for immediate action… Yes Ma'am… No problem... I'll talk to my daughter and one of us will be right over."

Paula hung up the phone and filled Lindsey in on the details.

"That was Ms. Evan's. Her two teenage sons started a fight with several other kids at school today. They've been suspended for 3 days. She wants them thoroughly punished as soon as possible."

"I'm on it!" Lindsey smirked, then added her humor. "Hell, I already have this strap in my hand!"

"Thank you, honey," her mom replied. "I'll text you her address."

"No rest for the wicked!" Lindsey chuckled, as she packed up the implements and headed for the door.

Just before she exited the house, she called out to her cousins.

"Girls, I'll see you at my house to help with the yard sale tomorrow morning... 9am... And don't even think about being late!"

I just wanted to take a moment to say Thank You for reading "". I hope you enjoyed this book and please by all means email me your comments.

As always I am truly grateful for your comments and positive reviews, as these are very helpful on all digital platforms.

Please feel free to say hi and join my mailing list at robinfairchild_author@yahoo.com. You'll receive FREE books and substantial discount promotions as well.

If you're a true spanking enthusiast, and love spanking as much as I do, then you will love reading my other books.

THE ACADEMY SERIES
Book 1 – Orientation
Book 2 – Kick-off Dance
Book 3 – Play Date
Book 4 – The Proposition
Book 5 – Lending A Hand
Book 6 – In Deep
Book 7 – Inappropriate Behavior
Book 8 – [1]Surprised Beyond Belief

THE SPANKING NEIGHBOR SERIES
The Spanking Neighbor
Uninhibited
The Spanking Neighbor – Book 2

The Spanking Neighbor – Book 3
The Spanking Neighbor – Book 4
The Spanking Neighbor – Book 5
The Spanking Neighbor – Book 6

Short Stories
Jordan's School Physical and Spanking
Julia's First Spanking
Julia's Coming Of Age Spanking
Locker Room Spankings
Spanked in Discipline Hall
Rebecca's Barn Spanking
Spanked In The Garage
Best Night Ever
A Lesson Learned
Attitude Adjustment
Spanked By The Coach
Caught, Searched, Spanked
A Kinky Afternoon (Also available in audio book)
The Stern Nurse
Crimson Bottoms

OTHER SERIES
Various Shades Of Spankings
A Spanking To Remember
Behaving Badly – Book 1

Please note: I release new books frequently. So, please check my website, as well as, your favorite book retailer often for my stories!

Printed in Great Britain
by Amazon

41810865R00136